Devils on Horseback: Lee

Look for these titles by
Beth Williamson

Now Available:

Devils on Horseback: Lee

Beth Williamson

SAMHAIN
PUBLISHING

Samhain Publishing, Ltd.
577 Mulberry Street, Suite 1520
Macon, GA 31201
www.samhainpublishing.com

Devils on Horseback: Lee
Copyright © 2011 by Beth Williamson
Print ISBN: 978-1-60928-073-4
Digital ISBN: 978-1-60928-044-4

Editing by Sasha Knight
Cover by Scott Carpenter

First Samhain Publishing, Ltd. electronic publication: May 2010
First Samhain Publishing, Ltd. print publication: March 2011

Dedication

To the Bradford babes, the most amazing, supportive, smart, talented and funny group of women I have ever had the privilege of knowing. Y'all rock.

Prologue

March 1867

Lee Blackwood frowned at his reflection in the window as the errant curl stuck up on his forehead for the tenth time that morning. He licked his fingers and smoothed it down again, yet the blond shock of hair had other ideas and sprang right back up.

"Damn."

"Don't you look beautiful?"

Lee whirled to find his cousin Gideon standing at the door, smirking, his arms folded across his chest.

"Shut up."

"You're sure all fancied up, Lee. And last time I checked, they hadn't moved Sunday to Tuesday. That means you're looking dapper for something other than the good reverend's sermon." Gideon stepped in, then walked around, assessing Lee's appearance. "Even wearing clean britches."

"I said shut up." Lee turned back to the window. "There's no call to tease me about it."

"Oh but there is." Gideon sounded amused. "Who else is gonna do it? Your brother is happily married and isn't around to do the job. That only leaves me as the closest relative."

Lee grumbled under his breath, but didn't give Gideon the

pleasure of hearing it.

"You know if you put a mirror in here, I wouldn't have to fix your hair." Gideon stepped over and reached for Lee's head.

He couldn't help flinching—even more than two years after the war ended. War changed a man, sometimes on the inside just as much as on the outside. Lee was no exception. His cousin stopped in mid-motion, waiting with concern evident on his face.

"Sorry." Lee let out a huge breath, wishing like hell he could be someone who didn't flinch away from people's touch.

Gideon slowly lowered his hands to Lee's head and fussed with his hair briefly, then stepped back. "God only knows why he put such a beautiful head of hair with such an ugly face." With a grin he patted Lee on the shoulder.

Lee snorted and grabbed for Gideon's brown curls. "At least I don't have a moppet head."

Gideon frowned and harrumphed. "I do not have a moppet head."

"And I do not have an ugly face." Lee moved what was left of his arm. "I do, however, have a hell of a scar to impress the girls with. Wish me luck, cousin."

He was nervous as hell, but had finally found the balls to do what he'd wanted to for quite a while. With more than a little trepidation, Lee Blackwood headed out the door, brushing past Gideon.

Quite possibly the rest of his life waited for him, he only had to get there.

His heart beat steadily as he waited. Lee had never considered himself a coward, but staring into the brown eyes of the woman he'd just proposed to had him quaking in his boots.

The light from the sun began to fill the restaurant. It was early, just past dawn, and they were the only two people downstairs. Gideon was still upstairs, leaving Lee alone with Margaret.

He'd fallen in love with her over time. It wasn't until his brother, Zeke, had pointed out the obvious affection that Lee realized what he was feeling was love. He'd been pushing people away for so long, what he experienced was foreign and scared him. After seeing the joy Zeke, Nate and Jake found with the women they loved, well, Lee thought it was time he acted on those unfamiliar feelings and maybe find a piece of that joy himself.

Margaret was a war widow, as were many women in Tanger, Texas. She'd been working for the restaurant co-owned by Lee, Zeke, Gideon and Cindy Cooley, who spent her days hiding in her now seemingly permanent room at the mill. The daily operations had been the Blackwoods' responsibility since it reopened six months earlier.

When Margaret first started working for them, Lee didn't want anything to do with her. Women had been scarce in his life, and since he'd lost most of his left arm in the war, they were even scarcer.

Yet she'd grown on him, the way she bossed him around, didn't take any of his guff or rudeness. Margaret treated him as if he was normal, and for that he'd fallen head over heels for her. It just took him a while to figure it out.

"Did you just ask me to marry you?" Margaret tucked a wisp of hair behind her ears. He tried not to notice that her hand shook.

Lee resisted the urge to squirm in his seat. "Well, yeah, I did." His cheeks felt warm and he knew he was probably blushing, but damn it, he couldn't help it.

11

She nodded and picked up the mug in front of her. The steam from the rich brew curled around her delicate features. "Why me?"

"Why not? We rub along good together." His stomach rolled into a ball at his cowardice. Lee could not tell her he loved her. Jesus, what a fool he was.

"Lee, you and I, we're friends." She shook her head slightly and his breath caught. "But I don't think we should be husband and wife."

At that moment, he couldn't swallow even if he wanted to. His mouth had gone as dry as trail dust. "Lots of folks start off as friends when they first get married." The words sounded thick and unnatural as his tongue tried to work properly.

When Margaret used the word "but", Lee knew he'd made a big mistake. Possibly the stupidest mistake of his life. Anger bubbled up inside him at his own foolishness.

"Then get it over with and say no." His head began to throb even as his hand clenched into a fist. "No woman wants a one-armed husband."

Her eyebrows slammed together. "Don't be ridiculous. I wouldn't care if you had one eye and a wooden leg. I don't judge people by the way they look."

"You're still going to say no." He stood and looked down at her. "I'm sorry I bothered you, Margaret. I wish— Damn, there's not enough hours in the day for that list."

As he walked away, he felt her gaze on his back and he nearly missed a step. Pain was not an unfamiliar emotion, but it sure as hell was an unwelcome one.

"Lee?"

He stopped, but didn't turn around. He couldn't. "What?"

"If I hadn't fallen in love with Matthew, I would have said

yes."

Matthew Marchison owned the mercantile in town, and he had both arms. Lee couldn't help the snort that burst from his throat. "Yeah, pardon me if I don't believe you."

She sighed softly. "Someday you're going to have to let go of that anger. If you don't, you'll never be happy."

This time he didn't stop walking. Lee burst from the restaurant and ran. He didn't know where he was running to, but he couldn't stay there even one more minute. Hurt and confusion wrestled with fury at God and frustration that he hadn't died on that battlefield.

No matter how far he ran though, he knew he'd never escape himself.

Chapter One

August 1867

Genevieve Blanchard had been blessed, or rather cursed, with a fancy name and not much else except an abundance of pride. It was that pride that kept her from asking for help for nearly six months after her no-account husband died.

Pride rode on her back as she made her way into town with a sullen Sophie beside her on the wagon seat. The seven-year-old took after her mama for sure.

"Now stop that bellyaching, Sophie. We need help and that's all there is to it." The words spilled out of her mouth, but they were hard to chew. Genny figured her daughter heard the doubt and latched onto it, like any stubborn female would.

"Not hardly. We can make do on our own. We have been since Pa died." Sophie pooched out her lower lip and frowned so fiercely her small eyebrows nearly touched. She favored her grandmother, like it or not. The wavy brown hair, the light blue eyes, even the heart-shaped face all screamed Camille.

Genny shook off the memories of her mother and focused on getting the old workhorse into town. Ned was twenty years old if he was a day, and every morning Genny wondered if he'd be standing or lying hooves up in his stall when she went to feed him.

"Git up there." She flicked the reins as they plodded along

toward Tanger. Genny aimed to ask for a little help, only a week or two's worth of work. She wasn't a charity case and wouldn't take help without something in return. If there was one thing she could do, it was sew really well. What she was hoping for was a single man who would trade some good hard work for new clothes. Much of Henry's clothes were salvageable, and since he was such a big man, she could make them fit just about anyone with a bit of work with a sewing needle.

"I still don't want to have a stranger at the farm." Sophie folded her arms. "Pa wouldn't like it."

Genny swallowed a snort. It didn't matter one whit what Henry would have thought of having a stranger help on the farm. As much as Genny loved Sophie, for certain there had been no love for the late Mr. Blanchard. He'd been a lazy man with three needs he constantly wanted satisfied. When Genny refused to provide one of those needs anymore, he went into town and found it at the whore's saloon. For that, Genny had been grateful.

Sophie was a blessing in a life spent with a man twenty-five years older than she was. However, she didn't want to have any more children. One was enough work considering Genny did the majority of the farm chores. Henry only worked when there were crops in the field. The other six months of the year, he sat on his ass and demanded to be serviced.

It was his laziness that convinced Genny she could manage the farm after his death. She had been doing everything herself already. She nearly laughed at the thought now. Little had she known just how wrong she'd be.

Shaking off the maudlin thoughts of her failures as a farm owner, Genny focused on Ned's hindquarters. No need to be crying over spilled milk. What she needed was to stop whining and realize although she didn't want help, she sure as hell needed it.

As they crested the last hill into Tanger, Genny's courage tried its best to jump ship. She gritted her teeth and forced herself to keep going. What kind of example would she give Sophie if she gave up because of her pride?

Through conversations she'd had with neighbors at the last shindig in town a few months ago, she heard the men from Georgia were still doing work for folks who needed it. She hadn't met any of those men except for the redheaded one who had married Gabby. It stood to reason that Genny could talk to Gabby about her needs at the farm. Asking for help would be a simple business transaction, nothing more.

Then why did Genny feel sick to her stomach?

Ignoring her breakfast churning around inside her, she headed straight for the mill. Although it wasn't busy this time of year, she knew Gabby was usually there.

"Where are we going, Mama?"

"To see Miss Gabby and get some help for the farm."

"But we don't need—"

"That's enough, young lady. Whether or not you realize it, we need help, and sometimes you have to accept the kindness of strangers even if it sticks in your craw." Genny hadn't meant to be so harsh, but judging by the look on Sophie's face, perhaps the girl would finally accept the inevitable.

Genny wondered if she'd been talking to herself or Sophie.

"After we see Miss Gabby, can we go to the store for a peppermint?" Sophie turned her gaze up at Genny. The girl knew how to manipulate with those wide, innocent eyes, smart little booger.

"If you behave yourself, then maybe. Mr. Marchison might have a penny candy or two he could part with." Genny was rewarded with a whoop of childish enthusiasm.

"Oh he always has peppermints, Mama. His little boy loved them so he gives them out to other young'uns. That way it reminds him of his own little boy." Sophie's explanation was simple, but the reasons for Matthew's generosity were much more complex.

Genny knew the man was trying to make amends for his wife's perfidy years ago when she had profited from kidnapping and selling the women in town. He also had lost his son in the war, and grief was a constant companion for the soft-spoken man.

When they pulled up to the mill, Genny realized her hands were shaking right along with the rest of her. She hadn't considered the possibility that no one would be available to help her, which meant she would have to hire a farmhand. They could little afford to pay anyone. Hell, they could hardly afford to feed themselves. Thank God for a big garden and the apple orchard.

Her feet hit the ground and she pulled up her courage from somewhere near her toes. With each step she took, Genny's throat grew tighter.

"Stay in the wagon while I find Miss Gabby."

Wisely, Sophie nodded and clutched the rag doll Genny had made for her when she was born. Genny was blessed to have what she did, and she intended on keeping it all for Sophie. If they could hang on to the farm, she would inherit it and hopefully spend her life there with her own family.

Squaring her shoulders, Genny stepped up on the porch and walked into the mill.

Lee watched the wagon, pulled by the oldest horse he'd ever seen, stop in front of the mill with a woman and girl on the seat.

He didn't know either of them, but the girl looked vaguely familiar. Maybe he'd seen her at the Founder's Day celebration in the spring.

He stood looking out the window waiting for Jake and Gabby to return. They had gone to see Doc Barham and asked him to keep an eye on her father. The man was bedbound and couldn't speak, but Lee did what he could to help considering he was living at the mill without paying room and board.

It had been months since Lee had been in the restaurant. He spent his days doing accounts for businesses in town, including the restaurant, and his meager pay went into the bank. His friend Richard Newman assured him that within six months he'd have enough to buy his own place.

Lee craved the isolation of his own home, away from the noise and drama of other people. Each time Gideon brought the receipts to him, he asked when Lee would return to the restaurant. Of course, the answer was never. There was no need to live at the restaurant when he could do his accounting work anyplace.

This allowed him to stay away from Margaret and keep his sanity. Gideon accepted his decision, but that didn't keep him from nagging at Lee almost every day.

The woman from the wagon stepped into the mill and Lee turned to face her. He wasn't sure what he expected, but when she took off her hideous bonnet, her youth surprised him. She was younger than he was.

Her skin was the color of cream with a touch of honey mixed in. A smattering of freckles stood out on her long, thin nose. With reddish brown hair captured in a bun on the back of her head, she was average looking, almost plain. However, she had a forthrightness in her brown gaze that gave him pause. Not many women were able to do that.

"Is Gabby here?" Her voice was like whiskey, husky and throaty with a slight rasp that immediately made the small hairs on his body stand up.

What the hell was that about?

"No."

She frowned and tried to peer into the depths of the mill. "Is she coming back soon?"

"Don't know."

"I have some business to talk with her about." She scrunched the bonnet in her hands as she waited for Lee to respond.

He didn't know why he was being rude. The woman had been polite and it wasn't her fault that her voice did strange things to him. That didn't stop him from being an ass, apparently. Lee brought his mother's face to mind and tried to remember to be a gentleman, at least for his mama's memory.

"She and Jake went to the doc's. You can wait for her there." Now that was a good suggestion. If he were lucky, she'd take it.

"No, I can't do that. I'll be right back." She went back out the door and Lee wondered what she was doing.

When she came back inside with the little girl, he almost choked on his own spit. He wasn't good around children, never was and likely never would be.

"My daughter and I will wait here for Gabby."

The girl took after her mother a bit, but in an awkward knobby-kneed, buck-toothed way. Her hair was in two braids, but it was so thick, there were pieces sticking out every which way. She looked around the room, then at him and what was left of his arm.

"Mama, that's the man who could shoot real good."

Now the girl had surprised him too. He hadn't even remembered the shooting contest at the Founder's Day celebration. Too many things had happened since then, but she obviously remembered him.

The woman's worried gaze dropped to his hips, likely expecting a gun to be hanging there. He almost snorted at the thought. It had been a long time since he carried a pistol every day.

"Hush. Don't be rude now." She nodded at him. "I'm Genevieve Blanchard, and this is my daughter, Sophie."

Lee stared at her, consistently surprised by how much her voice affected him. If she had decided to be a whore, the men wouldn't care what she looked like as long as she talked to them in bed. Not only that but she had a fancy French name too. Jesus, it was unnerving.

When she turned away to stand near the door, he realized he hadn't introduced himself because he'd been staring at the woman like a fool.

"Sorry, ma'am, my mind wandered there. I'm Lee Blackwood."

Genevieve reached out to shake his hand. "Pleased to meet you, Mr. Blackwood." Her grip was as strong as expected for a woman who looked like she worked hard.

Lee didn't know what to make of this woman. She was as plain as prairie grass, but she had bits and pieces that were extraordinary. All of it put together made him want to know more and at the same time, run the other direction.

"You can come sit in the kitchen if you'd like. I just made a fresh pot of coffee." Now his mouth had taken over and invited her in. Just like that. Damn fool tongue had apparently made his decision already.

She stared at him for a few beats, peering into his eyes as if she could see into his soul and determine if he was lying. "I'd be much obliged. The ride in was long and dusty."

Lee turned and walked toward the kitchen in the back right corner of the mill. It was the only living quarters downstairs and had a homey feel to it. The morning sun had warmed it up nicely and the smell of coffee permeated the air. It felt like a home to him, something he hadn't experienced in some time.

Too bad it wasn't his home.

The kitchen was as neat as a pin. Gabby was amazing—running a mill and keeping the house in order was no small task. The oblong table was covered in a green cloth Jake had given her for Christmas. Lee gestured to the woman and the girl.

"Please go ahead and sit. I can probably rustle up some milk for your daughter."

For the last few months, Gabby had been on a milk binge. In fact, every other day, they got a milk delivery from a farmer just outside of town in exchange for one five-pound bag of flour a week. Jake had built a small milk shed right outside the back door. He'd diverted some of the river water into the bottom of the shed. The cold water then surrounded a metal tub where the milk cans sat. Ingenious really, and it kept the milk nice and cold.

Lee had never been one to drink milk much, but having it cold made a difference. Of course he only drank it around Jake and Gabby. Grown men just didn't drink it like a baby. As he poured a glass, he considered taking a sip, but didn't want a milk mustache or anything. The woman and her daughter were already watching him, he didn't need to give them more ammunition.

By the time he stepped back into the kitchen, he felt calmer. He wasn't used to strangers, and he sure as hell didn't like to be around them more than absolutely necessary. Genevieve was sitting at the table talking quietly to the girl, who had her lower lip stuck out. He wondered what had set wrong with the little one, but not enough to task. It was bad enough he'd let them in and offered them a drink. He didn't need to know anything else about the child.

He set the milk down and stepped toward the stove. "It'll just take a minute to get the coffee."

"I already did."

Lee turned and saw two twin mugs of steaming coffee on the table. That was something he hadn't expected at all.

"I'm used to doing chores and it didn't seem right to make you wait on us, seeing as how we're waiting on Gabby." Genevieve shrugged. "I appreciate your hospitality."

"So is it because I would have had to make two trips to bring the coffee to the table?" As soon as the words left his mouth like a black cloud, Lee could have kicked himself.

She blinked twice before she spoke. "I hadn't thought about it. I was just doing what I always do."

Hidden behind her brown eyes he spotted a wary honesty. Sometimes he let his mouth loose and it made him look like a huge ass. This was no exception.

"You could use a tray to carry things." Genevieve pulled a cup toward her. "That way you don't need to make two trips."

Lee opened his mouth to speak then closed it again. She was right, of course, but the idea of using a tray had never occurred to him. Losing his left arm was not new, more than two years ago now, yet he still woke up at least once a week with an itch he could never scratch.

"I reckon you're right." He sat down with a thump across from her, cursing himself for having such a short fuse. He'd always had a problem keeping it under control, and losing his arm made it worse. His friends were the only ones who tolerated his outbursts, and sometimes they lost patience with him.

Lee picked up the cup and glanced at her. "Thanks."

She pursed her lips and nodded. "You're welcome."

He should have been a bit more gracious, but he didn't even know her. Gabby would kick his ass if she knew how he was behaving.

"Are you from around here?" There, that was polite.

She stopped, cup halfway to her mouth. Her lips were a deep shade of pink like the roses old Hettie grew outside her house in town. Just another feature of Genevieve that set him off balance.

"No, not originally." Her accent was smooth, almost melodic.

Lee focused on trying to remember where he'd heard it, because it for damn sure wasn't a Texas accent.

"We live on a farm and we don't need no man to help us." Sophie glared at him from over the top of the glass of milk, a white mustache sitting above her lips.

"I wasn't offering," he shot back.

If he didn't know any better, he'd have sworn Genevieve smiled behind her coffee cup.

"Mind your manners, Sophie. We're here to see Miss Gabby, not Mr. Blackwood." When she leaned down to speak to her daughter, a curl sprang free from her hair and swung back and forth against her cheek.

Lee almost choked on his coffee when the urge to feel that curl raced through him. He covered his idiocy by clearing his throat and willing away the wayward thoughts.

He grasped at any topic of conversation to distract him.

"How do you know Gabby?"

"My husband always brought the wheat crop to the mill." Genevieve returned her focus to him.

Good thing she had a husband, made things a bit less stressful for Lee.

"Gabby was always here and since we're about the same age, we visited when Henry and me came to town." Her finger circled the rim of the coffee cup and Lee couldn't help but notice the nails were clean and short, the fingers long and supple. He was startled to note there was no wedding ring on her left hand. Damn.

"Where's your husband now?" He was embarrassed to realize his voice broke on the last word. Hell, he was an idiot asking a question he had no business asking.

"He died." She glanced at Sophie with affection evident on her face. "Almost six months ago."

This time when her gaze met his, Lee felt a spark jump between them and the air grew heavier. Genevieve was a naturally sensual woman. For reasons he didn't want to contemplate, he was attracted to her. If he didn't know better, he might also believe she was attracted to him. Unlike her daughter, who was still shooting daggers at him with her eyes.

"I'm sorry to hear that." Oh how he lied.

"Thank you. Henry was, uh, well, he gave me Sophie and a farm to run." Genevieve let out a short laugh without much humor. "That's what I need to talk to Gabby about. I need a man."

Lee's mind raced with various images of what Genevieve would look like nude on his bed. Shit, he was already getting hard. What the hell was wrong with him? It was no business of his who climbed into her bed or why she needed a man.

When he heard footsteps on the porch, he jumped out of his chair, startling Genevieve and Sophie. "I'll be right back."

Lee exploded out the door and slammed into Jake. The redheaded man grabbed Lee's shoulders as he fell forward, stopping him from landing face first on the porch.

"Jesus Christ. What are you doing?" Jake steadied both of them before letting go of Lee.

Gabby stepped up beside them with both eyebrows raised. "Are you both okay?" Her long wavy black hair was in a fat braid lying over one shoulder while her hand rested on her stomach.

"I'm fine, but Lee looks like he saw a ghost." Jake smiled and patted Lee's shoulder.

"There's a woman in there waiting for you. She needs a man and I need to get some air." Lee pushed past them and headed to the waterwheel. He wasn't kidding when he said he needed air. Just the thought of being with a woman, with Genevieve, made him break out in a sweat and get lightheaded.

The sound of the river rushing past the mill called to him. Lee continued on toward the bank and breathing room. Perhaps when he returned, the woman who'd knocked him sideways would be gone.

"She needs help."

Lee looked up from the accounting ledger at Gabby. She leaned against the doorframe, a frown on her face.

"Who?"

"You know who. Genevieve Blanchard." She stepped into the room and sat across from him at the table. "Her husband died a few months ago, after he got the crops planted. She

25

thought she could handle the farm alone, with a seven-year-old child to help, but now that it's nearly time to bring the wheat in, she's finally asking for help."

Lee didn't want to talk about Genevieve. The woman had set him off balance the entire time she was at the mill. God only knew how odd things would have gotten if Gabby and Jake hadn't arrived home. All he wanted to know was that he didn't have to be around her any longer. Her voice still echoed in his head, dammit.

"I want you to help her."

Gabby's words fell like a boulder in a still pond, the ripples fanning outward getting larger and larger. Lee's mouth fell open as he stared at her, wondering if maybe he was dreaming.

"What?"

"I agree with her." Jake stepped into the room and for once, did not have a smile on his freckled face. It was an unusual occurrence to see him without that smile, which sent a chill up Lee's spine.

"Have you two gone loco? I can't help her." He raised what remained of his left arm. "Remember this? Cripples can't be farmers."

"Lee, you are the perfect person to help her." Gabby reached for his hand, but he dropped the pencil and pulled back before she touched him.

Panic bubbled in his stomach as Lee realized Jake and Gabby were serious. "I can't do shit on a farm. Jesus, I couldn't even wash the damn dishes at the restaurant."

"Those are your own perceptions, not what you can do if you put your mind to it." Gabby appeared to have lost all reasonable sense. "With effort, you can do anything. Look, you're a strong man with a strong back and damn smart too."

Lee snorted. "Jake, your wife is crazy."

"No, she's not. If you'd stop hiding behind that stump, you'd realize she's right." Jake didn't normally sound harsh or angry, but this time Lee heard both emotions in his friend's tone. "We took you in because you needed a place to be away from the restaurant and we respected that. It's been almost six months and it's time to move on, to discover what you can do. Hell, you didn't even know you could balance accounts until a year ago."

Lee surely didn't like the direction the conversation was heading. He stood, pushing the chair back so hard it fell with a crash. "I can't be a farmhand and that's that. Stop harping on me and you sure as hell better stop judging me."

"We're not judging you, Lee." Gabby looked up at him, sincerity in her voice even he couldn't dismiss. "We're trying to help two people at once."

Oh, he knew who the two people were, he just didn't want to hear it. Genevieve Blanchard was dangerous, and her daughter was likely a little hellion. No way he'd want to help them even with two arms. "There has to be someone else in town to help her."

"Who? You know perfectly well the men who live in Tanger. Most of them are old or can't possibly leave their jobs to help her. Zeke is the sheriff, Gideon runs the only restaurant, Richard runs the bank, Matthew the store, and Martin is the only blacksmith in fifty miles. There is no one else unless we trust a cowboy from one of the outlying ranches, which is like handing her and Sophie to a wolf."

Damn. She was right about that—Tanger had a very small population of men who were reliable and honest, not to mention under the age of sixty. The cowhands were a transient bunch, moving in and out with the seasons. Not a one of them was worth a spit.

"Don't make me do this," popped out of Lee's mouth. He beat back the urge to plead—no way he'd allow that to happen.

"We won't make you do anything." Jake sat beside Gabby and glanced at her. "But there's something we need to tell you."

Lee's heart thumped loud enough to make blood whoosh past his ears. Whatever they were going to tell him, it wasn't going to be good. He was already in a mood to get the hell out of there permanently. But where would he go? He couldn't go back to the restaurant. Zeke and Naomi lived above the sheriff's office in one little room. Richard might let him stay at his house, but Lee didn't want to accept his friend's charity. He was trapped by his own inability to be a man and find his path in the world.

"Out with it so I can decide whether or not to run."

Jake smiled. "It's not bad news." He leaned over and planted a loud kiss on Gabby's cheek. "We're going to have a baby."

Chapter Two

Genevieve unhooked the horse's traces while she mulled over her conversation with Gabby. Relief had mixed with shame when she accepted her friend's offer to find a man to help her with the harvest and the other chores around the farm. Sophie didn't speak a word on the way home—the girl had far too much sass in her already, or perhaps the half a dozen peppermints in her hand kept her quiet. Later on Genny would have a talk with her daughter about her runaway mouth.

Henry would not have allowed either of them to talk back without a slap upside the head. Since he passed, Sophie had been like a mini tornado let loose on the world, wild, untamed and unstoppable. Genny knew she should yank in the reins on her daughter, but after living under Henry's firm hand for almost eight years, the taste of freedom was very sweet for both of them.

He had left the farm in dire straits and Genny felt every painful second of every day as the harvest time grew closer. If they didn't bring in the crop, there would be no money for the winter. If he hadn't been such a lousy husband and farmer, the farm might have been in better shape. However, Henry was a foolish man with a penchant for poker and a lazy streak a mile wide. Genny was glad he was gone, even if it was wrong to speak ill of the dead. It was too bad her husband hadn't been like Lee Blackwood.

Henry had nothing in common with the stranger. Genny mentally catalogued the two of them and Henry sure came up wanting, even if Lee was missing an arm. He was handsome as sin, with chocolate brown eyes topped by lashes longer than any man should have. His shoulders and chest certainly marked him as a man who worked, as did the calluses on his hand.

Genny sighed. Why did her foolish mind keep circling back to Lee? She didn't need a man in her life, that was for certain, except for help around the farm. Yet his behavior had taken her aback, not an easy task for someone with her background. The man had one arm and he seemed to act as if he were not only angry about it, but wanted to let everyone know. The fact she'd surprised him by serving coffee was also a bit odd.

He was different, intriguing and dangerous, not to mention sinfully sexy. A combination Genny desperately needed to avoid.

So why in the world was she still thinking about him? Because she was aroused, that's why. He stirred her lust like a blond god, enough to make her damp between her thighs. Another momentous feat considering Genny had never liked sex with Henry. He was as selfish and boorish about that as he was about everything else. He made sex into a chore Genny tried to avoid as much as possible. She'd discovered ways to pleasure herself instead, given her wealth of knowledge learned in her less-than-normal childhood home.

She loved her daughter with a fierceness she hadn't known she had. However, Genny hadn't ever wanted to have a child with Henry. There were a lot of tricks her mother had taught her to prevent a baby, so luckily Genny had successfully avoided that possibility again. Sophie was all she needed. She wouldn't trade her daughter for even a second of time away from Henry—Sophie was a gift Genny treasured.

Too bad Lee hadn't been the first man between her legs. Perhaps then Genny might have enjoyed sex. Oh sweet heavens, that was the truth. He probably had that blond hair on his muscled chest that led down like a trail of treasure into his—

"That man, how did he lose his arm, Mama?"

Sophie's appearance startled Genny so bad she dropped the traces on her foot. Holding in the curses that threatened, she hopped up and down, red-faced and annoyed at herself. Her daughter picked up the traces and hung them on the peg on the wall.

"Sorry if'n I scared you." She sounded very contrite.

"It's okay, Sophie. I was woolgathering and should've been paying attention." Genny rubbed her foot, sure she'd probably done more than bruised it. Damn it, she was actually fantasizing about Lee's prowess in bed and how his body would feel beneath her hands.

"So how did it happen?"

"What? How did what happen?" Genny limped as she led old Ned to his stall. It was time to start paying attention to what she was doing.

"The man's arm." Sophie followed along behind, careful to avoid any piles left by the old horse. "What happened to it?"

Genny thought about the shadows lurking in Lee's eyes. There was definitely some ancient pain deep inside him. "I don't know, honey. Probably during the war. He has the look of a soldier. Very, ah, strong."

"He's strong? Even with one arm?" Sophie took a curry brush and started working on Ned.

For all the trouble she caused in the last six months, Sophie was still a good girl who took her responsibilities seriously. It was rare that Genny had to remind her to do her chores even if she complained loudly about it half the time. Sophie was a walking contradiction Genny didn't have the wherewithal to solve at the moment. Hell, she could barely focus on what she had to do.

While she put fresh feed in Ned's bucket, Genny contemplated how to answer Sophie. Although the girl had not known anyone without an arm before, her question was an honest one.

"He looks strong to me. And I think that when folks lose something, they tend to make it up in other places. Like Mr. Blackwood. He's likely very strong with his right arm." Genny leaned against the stall door and watched her daughter curry the horse.

After finishing with Ned, Genny and Sophie headed to the house with the late-morning sun burning brightly in their eyes. Genny was exhausted from the anxiety of the day, yet dinner and getting the room ready for whomever Gabby convinced to help them awaited her. Sophie could help, but the girl looked as tired as Genny felt.

"Why don't you go lie down, sweetie? I'll wake you when it's time to eat." She opened the door and ushered Sophie in.

"I'm not a baby, Mama. I don't need a nap." The girl let loose a jaw-cracking yawn.

"I know, but I need quiet. You'd be doing me a favor." Genny sighed with a bit more gusto than needed. "That drive plumb wore me out."

Sophie looked at her dubiously. "Not sure if you're fibbing or not, but I'll go lay down so's you can have quiet."

Lord, the girl was too stubborn by half. If someone told Sophie the sky was blue, she might have to argue with them. Genny shook her head and grabbed the bucket by the door. She had to wash some vegetables for dinner as well as her face and hands. The dust and dirt from the road coated her skin.

After getting water from the well, Genny took potatoes, turnips and carrots from the trapdoor under the kitchen. Performing a normal chore like making a meal helped to calm her frayed nerves. She only had a month until it was too late to bring the wheat in, then it would rot out in the fields and that possibility scared the hell out of her.

Lee stared out at the water as it rushed past the mill, the sound of the wheel making a thunderous noise even louder than the river. The spray from the water cooled his face, giving him a chance to catch his breath. Not only were Gabby and Jake pushing him to help the Blanchard woman, but they were going to have a baby.

That meant the bedroom Lee currently slept in would be needed for the child. Certainly they wouldn't move him in with Gabby's father—the man was an invalid. Then there was the reclusive Cindy Cooley, who'd barely left her room since she entered it a year and a half ago.

Lee occupied the room which at one time was probably a closet, but it was private and gave him the home he needed when he needed it. Now he'd been given a choice—to either leave before there wouldn't be a place for him or wait until they were forced to kick him out.

No way in hell he wanted to be in that position. He had too much pride for that, and damn sure he didn't relish being the unwanted guest with no place to sleep. Just the thought of being a nuisance to Jake and Gabby made his stomach clench.

There wasn't a choice—he had to leave.

Before he could change his mind or even think too hard about what he was doing, Lee headed back into the mill to pack. While he was gathering his few clothing items, strop and razor, and his other meager possessions, Lee realized he really had nothing. After the war, when they discovered Briar Creek had been destroyed, he and the Devils only had the clothes on their backs.

For Lee, he'd accumulated a whole lot of nothing since then as well. The only things he truly cared for were the men he traveled with, and now he was alone. The thought was like a punch in the gut, hard and fast. He had to sit on the small bed while he absorbed the idea.

He knew he still had them as friends, but they'd come to a point in their lives, a crossroads of sorts, where they were no longer making the journey together. Aside from Gideon, who had a restaurant to run, the other Devils had found their mates and put down roots. Lee, on the other hand, was still like a puff in the wind, blowing this way and that.

He had no roots, no mate, no future and no left arm.

A wave of sadness roared through him, and damned if he didn't have to swallow back tears as his throat closed up with emotion. Lee prided himself on never giving into the melancholy that plagued many men during and after the war. Yet here he was wallowing in self-pity instead of getting on his feet and changing his circumstances.

At first, Jake might have had to convince Lee to go to the widow's ranch. However, now Lee made the decision to step up and become his own man, to grab the reins and choose a path. He had to stop floundering around—it had gone on for two years. He would help Genevieve Blanchard then set up shop in Tanger as the town's accountant. Not a job many men would take, but dammit a cripple didn't have many choices. He couldn't work as a wrangler, cowboy or any other job requiring two arms. Besides he was damn good with numbers and could make his way in life as an accountant.

Lee stood and picked up his saddlebags, finally ready to begin the rest of his life.

Genny didn't expect anyone at the farm that day. After all, she'd only gone to town that morning and surely Gabby hadn't found someone willing to help already, so when she heard the sound of a horse whinny, then Ned's response, she dropped the sewing and rose. The shotgun lay next to the door, loaded and ready. She picked it up, the weight comfortable in her hand, then went to the kitchen.

She peered out the tiny window in the kitchen and didn't see anyone. Her heart pounded a steady tattoo as her hand tightened on the barrel of the gun. The early afternoon sun spilled bright light into the front yard. A breeze kicked up a small dust cloud across the otherwise still afternoon.

Genny strained to hear sounds, and above the short bursts of her breath, she heard the sound of hoofbeats. They grew louder as whoever was on the horse got closer to the house.

Since Henry's death, Genny had dreaded the day a stranger would come to the farm and demand more from her than a meal. She knew how to use the shotgun and wasn't afraid to. Her worry was for Sophie and what would happen to her daughter if Genny were hurt or killed.

The horse's neigh startled her enough that she almost dropped the gun. She took a deep breath and leaned to the right to view the front of the porch. All she could see was the side of the horse with a man's leg and foot in the stirrup. He wore a pair of gray trousers with a faint trim down the side—an ex-Confederate soldier then.

It could be someone from Tanger, but it could also be a man who was desperate for anything he could get his hands on.

Glancing backwards at her daughter's room, Genny felt a surge of courage, or perhaps stupidity, and went to the door. As she turned the knob, her stomach clenched so hard she tasted bile, but she went outside.

At first the sun was in her eyes, but she quickly stepped to the right and got a bead on the man on the horse. She wasn't sure if it was relief or surprise coursing through her when she recognized the stranger was none other than Lee Blackwood.

The brim of his hat shaded his eyes, but she noticed the tightening of his hand on the reins as she stood there with a weapon aimed at him.

She slowly lowered the gun, letting him know the situation was in her control, not his. Genny learned long ago that men would take control of any situation if a woman allowed them to. She wouldn't be that kind of woman.

"Good afternoon, Mr. Blackwood."

"Miz Blanchard." He inclined his head. "Do you always greet visitors with a shotgun?"

His voice was hard, even a bit more than she'd expected. This was the man who had been in her thoughts since they'd met at the mill. The fact he'd been the one to appear at the farm made her pulse flutter.

"I'm a woman alone with a little girl. Would you expect me to not protect me and mine?" Genny stepped off the porch. "You're more than welcome here, so if you don't mind, get down off the horse before I get a crick in my neck looking at you."

She sounded annoyed, dammit, and she didn't want to. The man had caught her off-guard, when she was ready to do battle for her daughter, and remembering her reaction to him made everything whirl around inside her. Genny didn't like the feeling, and as much as she found Lee to be intriguing, there were more important things to worry about than him.

He frowned at her, but he dismounted in a smoother motion than she anticipated. Considering he only had half of his left arm, she expected him to be awkward, but he was anything but. He landed on the dusty ground and walked in front of the horse, leading him by the reins. As he stepped closer, Genny fought the urge to move back.

"For someone who's asked for help, your hospitality ain't the best I've seen." The words flowed from his mouth in a lazy southern drawl, but she heard the bite behind them.

"I have to do what I have to do, Mr. Blackwood. I was doing some sewing inside. Why don't you set your horse in the barn and come on in for a spell." She turned her back on him, not waiting for a response, and headed into the house.

Genny wasn't sure if she was hoping for him to follow her or praying that he got back on his horse and rode away.

Lee stared at her nicely rounded backside, annoyed, intrigued and, damn, aroused again. Genevieve Blanchard knew exactly how to confound him, that was for sure. He grunted as he tied off the horse's reins to the hitching post. He damn sure needed to get his thoughts in order before he followed her.

Prior to the war, Lee had been young enough to only have kissed a few girls. During the war, he lost his virginity to a camp whore in the middle of a thunderstorm. It was quick, dirty and the most erotic experience of his life. It was the first of many experiences with her. He was careful to let no one know of his obsession with Fiona, the woman who'd taught him how to be a man. She followed the camp as they moved through the muddy fields during the war.

Even Zeke didn't know the extent of Lee's relationship with Fiona. She insisted he tell no one about his regular visits since most of the time she didn't even charge him. It wasn't until she disappeared that Lee realized just how badly he'd fallen for her. Hell, he almost deserted the Army to look for her. He hadn't seen her since March 1, 1865, more than two years ago.

Sometimes at night, in his deepest dreams, he would think of her, the smell of her hair, the softness of her skin, the tang of the sweat on her neck. He would wake up shaking and sweating, aching for release in her welcoming body.

Yet she had vanished so completely, even the other women around camp denied knowing her. Lee always wondered what he'd do if she reappeared in his life. A fairy tale to be sure. Considering he was only half the man he'd been before the war, Fiona would likely turn away from him as had every other woman he'd been attracted to since he'd lost his arm.

That is, until he met Genevieve.

She had spoken to him as if having one arm was an everyday thing, as if he could adapt easily. The thought that she could be right never entered his mind. Genevieve didn't know one damn thing about losing a limb and couldn't possibly know how fucking hard it was. He'd come to the farm as a favor to Gabby and Jake, and to have the time to put his own life in order. The fact he was there to help the widow was secondary considering there wasn't much he could do.

With as much trepidation as curiosity, Lee stepped into the house. The interior was lit by a single window over the sink and a lantern on the table. Obviously Genevieve's husband hadn't thought windows were important in a house. Likely the man was too damn lazy to put them in or too cheap to pay for them.

The rich smell of food filled the air. She was definitely making some kind of stew for dinner, with potatoes and possibly turnips. His stomach picked that moment to rumble, and he hoped like hell she hadn't heard it.

Genevieve sat at the table, a blue shirt in hand with needle poised in the air. The thread was a slim connection between the needle and the fabric, glinting in the lamplight. A basket was beside her on the floor, with various shirts and trousers stacked in a neat pile. She gestured to the chair across from her.

"Please sit."

Lee took a second to review the layout of the house. Along with two closed doors and a large open room, it appeared to be a simple plan with only one entrance that also served as the exit. He pulled the chair to the side of the table so his back was to the wall, then sat down.

She raised one eyebrow at his behavior, but said nothing about it. "What brings you out here, Mr. Blackwood?"

He realized she wasn't going to make this easy, but then again, his behavior earlier didn't exactly speak of a polite welcome either.

"Gabby asked me to come," he blurted. Was there ever a time he could actually speak without making an ass of himself? "I mean, she told me about your situation and thought I should come out here and see if I could help." He shrugged. "I told her I didn't think I was the man for the job, but she and Jake do. Not much I can do on a farm, but I'm here."

She pushed the needle through the fabric a few more times before she spoke. "That's a flattering offer, Mr. Blackwood."

Was she being serious or did he detect sarcasm? He didn't know her well enough to tell.

"Did Gabby tell you what kind of help I needed?" she continued.

"Farm work, chores and such." Lee hadn't asked Gabby for more details and probably should have. Now he regretted that.

"It's a bit more than that. We've got to bring in the crop." She nodded in the direction of the window. "About one hundred acres worth. Without it, Sophie and I won't last the winter."

The very idea that this woman and her child's life depended on his ability to bring in a hundred-acre wheat crop made him break out in a cold sweat. He didn't want to be responsible for them, and he damn sure wasn't able to bring in that much damn wheat by himself.

Her husky voice stopped him before he could even move. "Before you run for the door, let me say something first." She set the shirt down on the table and folded her hands in front of her. "You would not be alone doing this. I have always helped Henry with the harvest. This farm is all I've got to give Sophie, and I intend on doing everything I can do to keep it running for her. I know this is a lot to ask of a stranger, but I will give you a room to sleep in while you're here, feed you whenever you're hungry and new clothes to take with you when you go."

Lee glanced at the shirt, realizing she wasn't mending it, but rather altering it. She'd already begun making him the clothes he'd take with him before he even said yes. Never mind all his worldly belongings were in the saddlebags outside, or that he'd already moved out of the mill. He wasn't sure he could do what she needed him to. No, he knew he couldn't do it.

"I appreciate the offer, Miz Blanchard. I'm not sure I can do much in a wheat field. I don't even have two hands."

"I've got two and between us, we've got three. There isn't anything you can't do if you've a mind to, Mr. Blackwood. I learned that at an early age running the streets of New O— Well, let's just say I'm not a quitter." Her gaze was steady and penetrating. "I won't beg though, so if you want to be on your way, then so be it."

He took in her earnest expression, the pride obvious in her tone and posture, and the fact she was alone, fighting for her daughter. Whether or not she'd ever worn a uniform, Genevieve

Blanchard was a soldier. He respected that more than anything.

"I guess you've got yourself a farmhand then."

When Genevieve smiled, Lee recognized he'd just set himself up to live in a house with a woman whose voice incited erotic fantasies and whose smile lit up a room.

Damn.

Chapter Three

Dinner might have been delicious, but Genny didn't enjoy it. The stew tasted like sawdust and her stomach jumped like a passel of frogs. Lee barely spoke two words and Sophie spent the meal staring daggers at the man.

It was a ridiculous mess of Genny's own making.

When he'd walked in the cabin, everything seemed to shrink. The man was big, bigger than she remembered, and damn but he smelled good. She breathed him in, a mixture of soap, man and outdoors. It was a heady combination, and much to her consternation, made her admit to herself that she was definitely attracted to him. That was something she didn't need, especially now when her future was so uncertain.

Genny probably should have simply accepted his denial of being able to work around the farm. It would have eliminated the discomfort of being attracted to someone she could never be with. The easy way out, but she didn't have that choice. The practical side of her took over and insisted she convince him to stay. She didn't fancy starving to death and losing the one good thing Henry had left behind.

Genny mechanically chewed the food while surreptitiously watching Lee out of the corner of her eye. He ate like a gentleman, never getting food stuck in the corner of his mouth or spilling it down his shirt. Someone had taught him amazing table manners, better than hers as a matter of fact.

His lower lip was slightly plumper than the top one, giving him the look as if he was ready to kiss someone. She tried to stop herself from fantasizing what it would be like to kiss him and failed miserably. It wasn't as if Genny hadn't been with a man before, but no man actually made her squirm in her darned chair.

"Mama, what are you doing?" Sophie's voice broke through Genny's cloud of stupidity.

"Hmm?"

Sophie scowled at her. "You were moaning like your belly hurt, then licked the spoon like we was making frosting or something."

Her cheeks heated with embarrassment. She couldn't possibly have been acting like that, no sir. After all, she had iron self-control that couldn't be broken by an attraction to a man she'd only just met. Not a chance.

"The stew is just so delicious." She managed a small smile. "I was real hungry after all the chores I did today."

Lee, bless his heart, didn't look up from his bowl. Thank God. It was bad enough Sophie noticed her behavior and pointed it out to all of them, but if Lee had been staring at her, Genny would have had to fire him before he even started working for her.

"I think it tastes like horse shit." Sophie threw her spoon on the table and stalked out the door, leaving Genny openmouthed and even more embarrassed than she had been.

She knew her daughter had been acting wild, but she hadn't expected the girl to start cussing like Henry had. Genny had already decided she needed to discipline the girl, and as anger pushed the shame aside, she rose to her feet to follow Sophie.

Lee's hand on her arm stopped her.

"Let her be. Girl is upset about me being here and taking her father's place working the farm. If you go fuss at her now, it'll only get worse."

Genny knew he must have certainly struggled because of the loss of his arm. Gabby told her he was a good man, but aside from that, she had known next to nothing about him. Until now.

In his eyes she saw so many things that it was difficult to take them all in. Pain so deep she nearly felt it herself, shame, guilt, and most of all, anger. In the corners, however, she saw tiny bits of hope, forgiveness and charity. Lee was no simple man with simple needs—he was as twisted up inside as she was. Likely take a bonfire to chase away all the shadows lurking in him.

It was unusual for a man to understand a little girl, doubly so considering he didn't know Sophie, and Henry never even came close to understanding in the seven years since her birth. Genny was almost overwhelmed with what she'd learned in the last sixty seconds about Lee Blackwood. She groped for the words to bring her focus back.

"I, uh, okay. You're right, of course. It's been a hard year for her, with losing her pa and all." If not a complete lie, then a partial one. "You been around young'uns much?"

Lee let her arm loose and the loss of heat made her shiver. He was so blessedly warm.

"Nope. I was the youngest in my family." He turned his attention back to the stew and didn't speak again for the rest of the meal, which was a good thing.

While he ate, Genny used the time to find her self-control. It had been quite a while since she'd felt the need to do so. While living with Henry, she either had to hang on with gritted teeth or lose herself completely. Lee, on the other hand, made her want to let all of her walls down. That could never happen.

She rose and started washing the dishes, not waiting to see if he was still eating or had left the table. There would be too many meals to count in the coming weeks and she shouldn't let herself get worked up over the man each and every time. He would be working for her, an employee, not a lover or friend. She had to keep that in her mind at all times.

Easier said than done of course.

When he stepped up beside her, silent as a cat, she jumped a good foot off the ground. His brows rose but he simply handed her a plate without commenting. No doubt the heat in her cheeks indicated she was blushing like a fool. Up close, she could smell him again, and it was somewhat intoxicating.

"I'll go get started in the barn." He disappeared before she could respond.

Genny reminded herself that farm chores were what she hired him for. Certainly she didn't need him to be in the kitchen underfoot and around her, confusing and arousing her.

She barely resisted the urge to follow him.

Lee couldn't wait to get the hell out of the house. The woman was odd, and the girl even odder. They gave him a damn eye twitch with all the strange goings-on. He wasn't about to attribute it to himself because aside from being an ex-soldier with a missing arm and a short fuse, Lee was normal. Genevieve and Sophie were beyond any experience he'd had and it made him off balance to be around them. Next time he went to town, he'd need to find out about her dead husband and see just how crazy the man had been.

The farm itself looked tired, hell even the buildings were sagging as if they needed a long rest. The only thing that looked in somewhat good shape was the barn. No doubt the man had horses he wanted to keep safe. Lee had known many men like that, ones who valued money above all else, including their flesh and blood. Gideon's pa had been such a man, a terrible uncle to Lee and Zeke, a worse father to Gid.

Lee stepped into the gloom of the barn after kicking the door twice to get it open. The smell hit him first—old shit and piss were hard to miss. His eyes watered and he turned to get both doors open before he ventured any farther into the building. There was a significant amount of scuttling, likely a colony of mice and critters making their home in the filth of the barn.

The wagon sat in the middle, leaving five feet on each side to walk. There appeared to be ten stalls and one horse all the way at the far end. By the looks of the bay, it was the ancient nag he'd seen in town pulling the wagon. He lifted his head and neighed softly as he saw Lee—the horse probably couldn't smell anymore or he would probably have refused to even enter the barn.

Lee walked down the length of the building toward the only occupant. He glanced in each stall as he passed, noting the mildew-covered straw and old piles of manure long since forgotten. One stall held two fresh bales of hay. The horse had a friendly disposition and nuzzled his great head against Lee's shoulder, breathing in his scent.

"You're a good boy, aren't you?" Lee petted his neck as the equine got to know him. "What's your name?"

"His name is Ned." The girl's voice almost made him jump. She was quiet as a cat in socks, for Pete's sake. Judging by her tone, she was just as obnoxious and sassy as she'd been earlier.

Lee smiled grimly at the horse. Little Miss Sophie had no idea who she was dealing with. When he turned to look at her, he put on his fiercest expression. "It's important to take care of your horse so he can take care of you. Does your mama know you don't keep this barn clean? Or that it smells worse than five outhouses put together? Does she know you keep moving Ned from stall to stall because you don't want to clean his shit?"

"That's none of your business."

She leaned against the wagon wheel, arms crossed, britches held up by a piece of rope. This one reminded him of Nate's Elisa—all piss and vinegar, ready to fight the world at the drop of a hat. For all the fighting he'd done with their dapper, well-spoken Devil, Lee found the memory of Nate made his throat close up. Damn, he never thought he'd miss the man who married the fiery-tongued Elisa and settled on their ranch a couple days east of them. Lee shook himself to get rid of the soft feelings for the natty Devil and focused on the girl in front of him. Somebody needed to paddle her little ass.

"It is if I'm to work for your mama. It smells in here and needs to be cleaned up so grab a pitchfork and a wheelbarrow. You need to earn your keep considering this is your mess." He saw the answer in her eyes before she even opened her mouth to speak. "Don't bother telling me I can't order you around. I sure as hell can. Your mama asked for help and I'm gonna give it. That starts with not taking any backtalk from a half-pint like you. Now get the damn pitchfork before I get it for you."

"We don't need no man 'round here." She pooched out her lower lip so far a bird could've landed on it.

"Too bad because you've only got me. Now git to work, girl." He didn't wait for her to obey, instead he turned his back and got busy himself. After he led Ned to join his horse in the sorry excuse for a corral—nearly half the boards were crooked and the other half missing—he went back inside the barn to find Sophie mucking Ned's stall.

"That's a start, but every one of these needs to be cleaned. Probably need to tie a cloth around our mouths because it's foul as hell in here." His eyes were already watering. How did they stand it?

"You shouldn't cuss around me. Mama says it ain't proper." She didn't look up from her task as she admonished him. The girl was a forty-year-old woman in the body of a seven-year-old.

"I ain't no gentleman so it don't matter one whit. Besides which, I heard you cussing not twenty minutes ago." He glanced around and spotted another pitchfork hanging on a nail near the door. Lee stared at it, remembering the painful attempts at using a pitchfork with one arm and just how frustrating it was. No help for it though, he was hired to work and that was that.

Half an hour later, Lee wanted to ride back to town. His back screamed for mercy as sweat ran in rivers down his face. He'd chosen the stall with the driest manure to begin since it weighed the least. He stuck the end of the pitchfork under his left arm, or the stump as he called it. Then, by gripping the wooden handle with his armpit, he could guide the implement to the pile and scoop a chunk of the horse shit and hay. Things appeared to be in good shape with the first attempt.

However, without two hands, hefting the full pitchfork into the wheelbarrow was more than difficult. He lost half of it trying to flip the pitchfork, and got at least half a dozen splinters in the skin under his shirt. Cognizant of the little ears in the barn, he cursed under his breath.

Jake was wrong, completely, utterly wrong. Lee couldn't do it. There was just no possible way he could be a farmhand when he couldn't even muck out the fucking stalls. How the hell was he supposed to do things like put in a fence post or hold a board to nail it in? He was crippled and nothing would change that, no matter how much he wished it would.

"You need a harness." Sophie's voice startled him yet again.

"What the hell are you doing?" He wiped his arm across his sweaty brow and tried to slow down his racing heart.

She looked dirtier than the floor with smudges of God only knew what on her face and arms. He reluctantly acknowledged she had been working, when he honestly expected her not to given the sass in her. "You need a harness, like Ned. He can't plow the field without a harness to hold the plow 'cause he ain't got no hands either."

Lee's face grew hot at the bald statement, but damned if the little imp wasn't right.

Genny crept into the barn with a bucket full of cool water in case her new employee was thirsty. Of course, she'd be lying to herself if she didn't admit she was really checking on Lee. She was afraid he'd run back to Tanger or maybe she wanted to be around him again. That thought made her almost blush. The soft murmur of voices came from the back of the barn as the stench of the mess made her eyes burn. She knew the barn needed work, a lot of it, and felt guilty each time she moved Ned to another stall, but there was only so much she could do. It really was embarrassing to have a stranger see how bad things had gotten on the farm.

Yet this was why she needed help and, grudgingly, a man's strength. Genny wasn't tiny, but she just couldn't pick up a fence post and put it in a hole, and she surely could not harvest acres and acres of wheat. Lee wasn't what she was expecting, but then again, he was working for next to nothing. He might not have two hands, but he had strength in abundance judging by the width and size of his shoulders.

When she walked nearer to the stalls, she heard Sophie tell him he needed a harness like the horse, and Genny's face heated. Oh hell, did the child have no manners at all? And whose fault was that? Certainly not Henry, he barely even looked at Sophie and had no hand in raising her.

No, the blame lay squarely on Genny's shoulders. Since Lee's arrival at the farm, nothing had gone right between the girl and the man—this was just another nail in Genny's coffin of bad choices.

Genny walked quickly toward them, her mind whirling with the right way to apologize for Sophie's too-honest ways. Mr. Blackwood had agreed to her terms of employment knowing she had a child, but it didn't involve her daughter's insults.

"You're right."

His softly worded response made her pause in mid-stride. Surprise kept her there.

"I am?" Sophie's tone was full of shock. "Mama usually tells me I'm wrong."

Genny grimaced, knowing that was a true statement. The girl usually had the craziest notions and she had to keep her feet on the ground. Dreaming and wishing weren't going to get her anywhere in life. Genny's life had gone completely sideways and she was determined her daughter would have better.

Pasting on a smile, Genny cleared her throat and walked toward them with enough noise they could hear her coming. No need letting him know she'd been spying on them, or rather eavesdropping. Some habits were hard to break, and she was no saint with her overabundance of flaws and vices. God gave her what He thought she needed and there was no changing it.

"I thought y'all might be thirsty." Genny's hand started to cramp from carrying the bucket. It was heavy but if she were honest with herself, she had been gripping it too tightly. Another sign that Lee put her off balance.

As she walked toward them she avoided looking into the

stalls—the smell told the story quite clearly. Lee and Sophie were down toward Ned's current stall, a wheelbarrow behind them mounded with horse shit and hay, some of which looked like it had white and green fur growing on it. Genny bit back the urge to make a face at what she'd allowed to happen to her barn.

Lee was looking down at the pitchfork, turning it back and forth in his hand while Sophie peered up at him with her brow furrowed. Neither one of them acknowledged her.

"Hello? Water?"

This time he must've actually heard her because his head snapped up and his gaze slammed into hers like a bullet. His brown eyes were full of pain and pride—a dangerous combination, one Genny knew too well.

"Thirsty?" she asked with forced cheer. Without waiting for a response, she brought the bucket over to him and set it on the floor. Glancing at his threadbare pants and noting they would be the first to get burned, she filled the dipper and held it up to him.

"I'm much obliged, Miz Blanchard." The sweet southern drawl fell so easily from his tongue, she wasn't sure it was as sweet as it sounded.

He brought the dipper to his mouth and Genny froze in place, mesmerized by the play of muscles, skin and lips as Lee drank the cool well water. As he tilted the dipper, drops ran out the sides of his mouth, then slowly dripped onto his chest.

She wanted to lick them off.

Damp blond curls peeped out from the opening in his shirt. The smell of the barn faded away as the scent of a man washed over her. She wasn't one to lose her head over a working man, or any man for that matter, but there was something about Lee that plucked her strings.

"Much obliged."

Genny realized he was holding the dipper out to her and she was standing there like an idiot. "Th-hanks. I mean, you're welcome." She threw the dipper back into the bucket at her feet, splashing water on both of them.

Jesus Lord, have mercy! Did she have even an ounce of grace around this man? When she peered up at his face, Genny swore his mouth twitched in a smile or maybe even a laugh.

"I'm sorry, Lee, I didn't—"

"What happened to calling me Mr. Blackwood?" This time there was no humor in his voice. It was low and sexy, a bedroom voice that raised an army of goose bumps up and down her skin.

Without thought, likely a good thing, Genny swayed toward him, pulled by whatever attraction drew them together. It was an elemental connection, something that felt as old as a river and as impossible to control. His nostrils flared as if he'd scented her as well. She felt like a bitch in heat.

Her breath came out in short bursts; she couldn't suck in enough air to fill her lungs. When she came within six inches of him, she could see just how beautiful his eyes were. A dark brown, they also had gold flecks embedded in them. Lee was like a secret mine in a mountain, rich with treasure but difficult to reach without tools and a hell of a lot of work.

Genny didn't seem to care about any impediments or even the fact she was about to kiss a man who was also her employee. Her eyes drifted closed as the heat from Lee's body permeated hers, raising her temperature too.

"Mama, I'm building a harness for Mr. Blackie." Sophie's voice was more shocking than if someone had thrown the bucket of water on Genny.

Judging by the startled way Lee stepped back a foot away

from her, it was just as shocking to him. What the hell had she been thinking?

"Blackwood, honey." Genny didn't like the way she sounded raspier than usual, but there wasn't a damn thing she could do about it without the aid of that cold water.

"So I told him he needed a harness like Ned." Sophie held up some old traces from Ned's former companion horse, Eloise. "Can't we make these into somethin'?"

Genny turned to Lee and tried to gauge his reaction to the suggestion. He shifted his weight and stared back at her with an intensity that saluted the goose-bump army.

"We can try if that's what Lee, I mean, Mr. Blackwood wants."

"What I want doesn't mean spit." He nodded toward Sophie. "The girl had a good idea so just do it."

Genny had no idea how to take tack from an old horse and transform it into something a man with one arm could use, but she was willing to try. Heck, she could sew anything, why not use that skill to make something that might help Lee. Perhaps she could even use material from Henry's old coat or maybe his canvas trousers. The possibilities for a woman with a sharp needle were endless, particularly if it was going to make his work easier.

She didn't think about the fact she'd have to be physically close to him to make the harness, or rather she kicked it to the back of her mind. A seamstress was a professional and didn't get distracted by the body in front of her.

Genny had all she could do not to snort. Distraction was the least of her worries—attraction was the biggest. Lee could have her in his bed in five minutes if he asked her. She wouldn't offer herself up to him, but if he did the asking, she knew for certain there would be no contemplation. There would only be action and reaction. Genny swallowed hard and willed her heart to stop beating as if she was in Lee's bed already.

Good God, had she no shame? Was she that much like her mother? Hopefully the answer to that was no. The last thing she wanted was to be a woman who gave up everything, including her life, for a man.

Genny took the traces from Sophie, surprised the small girl had carried the heavy leather and metal. "I will probably need to take some measurements from you although I'm pretty certain I already know how big you are."

This time, his mouth not only twitched, it formed a full-blown grin. Like a little boy who'd heard a naughty joke, or a man who'd just discovered a woman found him handsome as sin. In this case, possibly both.

Her own lips wanted to smile back at him, but she wouldn't allow herself that luxury. Lee was an employee, he worked for her, therefore she shouldn't even contemplate kissing him much less measuring the length of his dick.

That didn't stop her from wondering about it though.

She gestured toward the bucket. "I'll leave the water for you and, uh, get started on the harness. When you come in for supper, I'll take some measurements."

Genny backed away, the weight of the leather dragging her hands down. Lee watched her, reminding her of a great cat observing his prey trying to hide. That thought made her stop in her tracks.

She was not anyone's prey and she had to stop thinking of Lee as a predator. When she looked at him, really looked at him, she could see the frustration and pain on his face from the menial task made a million times harder because of his lack of two hands. Genny's imagination had conjured up bad intentions, something bound to make her run. When would she learn to trust her eyes instead of her memories?

"You okay, Miz Blanchard?" Lee frowned. "You're not going to have a fit of vapors or anything, are you?"

His question knocked the strangeness from the situation and prompted a snort to pop out of Genny. "Not hardly. Just feeling the heat, I guess." With a smile and a lighter heart, she turned to go. "I'll give y'all a shout when it's close to supper."

As she walked toward the barn door, she began chastising herself for being such a complete idiot. Lee's voice stopped her in her tracks.

"Miz Blanchard?"

She spoke without looking back. "Yes?"

"I, uh, thanks for, uh, working on the harness." His voice sounded strained as if expressing gratitude was something he didn't do often. It didn't surprise her; he didn't seem the type to say thank you easily. It meant, however, that he really was grateful.

"You're welcome, Mr. Blackwood. I am happy to do it." And she was, truly she was. Lee's help in getting the crop in was all that stood between her and starvation.

A little voice deep inside her reminded her that she was doing it for selfish reasons, using him for her own means. The stark truth, of course. She'd do anything she could to save the farm and her daughter. Her attraction to the man was of no consequence and would go no farther than her mind's meanderings.

It was a promise, or rather a vow, she made to herself as she went back to the house to make a harness for her employee.

Lee heard Genevieve call him over the roaring in his ears.

Exhaustion from working all afternoon had crept up on him, draining his energy until he was forcing himself to continue. The girl had given up two hours earlier and he encouraged her to go. The little thing was no bigger than a minute and couldn't work for six hours in a hot barn with moldy horse shit.

She had gumption, smarts and a tongue as sharp as his was. Sophie was going to make some man crazy when she grew up. That was a certainty.

"Ready for supper?" The imp appeared at his elbow without making a sound. He had all he could do not to jump a foot in the air.

Lee set the pitchfork against the stall wall, annoyed to see his hand shaking. "I'm dirtier than he—than a pig in a wallow."

"Mama set out some soap for you by the well pump." She peered at his face. "You're all red."

"I'm hot and tired, brat." He straightened, the muscles in his back screaming or perhaps crying at the movement. "Show me where the pump is."

"I ain't a brat." Nose in the air she led him out of the barn and around the side of the house. "Well's over yonder." She pointed to the right. "Mama's expecting you in ten minutes."

Sophie stormed off before Lee could even manage to say thanks, not that he would have anyway. The little thing needed a full-fledged soak in a hot tub to get rid of the snarls in the bird's nest she called her hair, and the dirt was permanently embedded on that neck, of that he was certain.

He wasn't one for long soaks, but a hot bath sounded pretty heavenly right about then. For most of his life, Lee was always busy doing something. He could never sit still for very long and found things to keep him occupied. Even after the war, when he was still getting used to one arm, he worked as hard as the rest of his friends at whatever shit job they happened to snag.

Yet ever since they finished the restaurant a year or so ago, he'd done nothing more than cook on occasion and do the accounting books, and sometimes ride. Working in the Blanchards' barn for half a day reminded him in no uncertain terms that he'd been sitting on his ass for too long. Lee was sorer than he ever remembered being in his life.

Shambling along like a sixty-four-year-old man instead of a twenty-four-year-old man, he found the well pump near the far corner of the house. Beside it was a crate turned on end with a bar of soap, a ratty-looking but clean towel, and what appeared to be new clothes.

It was the clothes that made his throat close up unexpectedly.

The shirt was a sky blue color, with tight, even stitches and a pocket on either breast. Shiny buttons that matched winked in the fading sunlight. The trousers were canvas made soft by many washings, but the stitching was impeccable and the buttons perfectly aligned.

Genevieve had done this. She'd made him new clothes— and not just the shirt he'd seen her stitching when he first arrived at the farm. It had been so very long since anyone had gone out of their way to make something for him and only him.

She couldn't have known he would arrive at the farm, yet she had started altering the clothes. Maybe he wanted to believe she hoped he would come. In the time he'd been there she finished the clothes and gifted them to him. To *him*.

Lee squatted beside the crate and pressed his forehead into the cool metal of the pump head. He swallowed twice to dislodge the lump in his throat. All his life, he'd been second or third on everyone's priorities, except for his mother's. She smothered him so much he couldn't breathe so he pushed her away. Zeke had even abandoned him when their father took ill, leaving Lee alone for years. Since no one seemed to give a shit what he did, he just did what he wanted and lived down to everyone's expectations.

That kind of choice had been his downfall in the war, the reason he'd lost his arm. Some would call him reckless and willful, and right about then he'd have agreed with them. He'd spent so much time being angry at the world, at God, and at everyone around him, Lee had passed up most chances at happiness. He was surprised how much his friends had put up with.

Fact was, he kept people at a distance to keep himself safe. Genny had just put a huge dent in the wall around him. Jesus, she'd even pinned up the left sleeve already.

He hung his head in shame as grief welled inside him, threatening to overwhelm him. The simple gesture by a not-so-simple woman had affected him greatly, more than he'd want her to know. Lee squeezed his eyes shut and tears burned the back of his lids. He concentrated on breathing in and out, until his emotions were slammed back behind the door inside his heart, until he felt more in control of himself.

As he rose to his feet and began stripping off his clothes, Lee reminded himself that his own sweat paid for those clothes and the gift was nothing more than payment for a job, whether or not it was well done.

Chapter Four

Genny had seen a lot of sights in her life, even naked men. Growing up in New Orleans gave her a bird's-eye view of things most folks wouldn't want to see. Her mother, Camille, had done what she thought was right to keep herself alive, no matter the cost. Genny happened to be an afterthought most of the time, which was okay with her because the men who frequented her mother's bed were not the kind Genny wished to know anyway.

A fallen mistress forced to sell her wares while she lamented her lost love, Camille Boudreaux was nothing more than a common whore, one who'd traded away her daughter for creature comforts to protect herself instead of her child.

Naked men were nothing new, nothing to even get too excited about. Or at least that's what Genny thought until she looked out the small window and saw Lee stripping off his sweat-soaked shirt. She hardly noticed the missing part of his arm because she was captivated by the body revealed in the fading evening light.

Dark sprinkles of blond hair, wet from the sweat, sparkled against the honey-gold expanse of skin. He obviously had scars, they stood white against the darker skin, but Lord help her, the man was beautiful.

Her pussy throbbed with arousal almost instantly, shocking her so much she dropped the pan of cornbread two inches away from her foot. Fortunately the bread was still intact for supper, even if her pride suffered from her body's shocking reaction. Granted, Lee hadn't stripped down completely, much to her disappointment.

She was still staring when he started walking toward the house. Genny busied herself putting supper on the table, but when he stepped into the kitchen, she couldn't help but glance at the snug fit of the trousers around his cock. The man was definitely well-endowed. He was dressed in the shirt she'd left him, looking as if he'd spiffed up to go to church. After mumbling a thank you, he sat at the table and waited to be served.

Genny forced herself to focus on the meal, yet when she joined him at the table, there was awkward silence again. If meals didn't improve, Genny might have to serve Lee separately to spare them all the discomfort.

Genny might have been upset with him for his brusque behavior, but she had a guilty conscience. After all, she'd been staring at him as he washed up. Not only that, but she'd enjoyed every second of it. Her body had reacted more strongly by just watching him than when she'd been touched by any man. That was very telling, and somewhat frightening.

Genny blushed with the memory of pressing herself against the wooden sink, enjoying the sensation, imagining it was Lee's hardness.

"Mama, you feel okay? Your face is mighty red." Sophie's voice broke her out of the memory.

"It was warm in here cooking, that's all." Genny forced a smile. "Now eat your supper. You worked hard today and need to have a good meal."

Genny's voice sounded stilted and forced, even to her own ears. Almost lazily, Lee lifted his head and looked at her. His intense stare sizzled across the table, raising goose bumps on her arms, and then her nipples hardened as well. This reaction was so far out of her normal one, Genny felt trapped by it. She'd grown up wise in the ways of men and women, but apparently ignorant of what happened in herself.

"Cornbread's good," he offered around a bite.

Genny, damn her stupid self, couldn't make her tongue form a proper thank you. She gestured to the pan, encouraging him to eat more.

"Thank you kindly, but I think this is all I need at the moment." His voice had dropped again, and the husky tone skittered across her skin like a caress.

"I want more." Sophie started to reach her hand into the pan, but Genny snatched her wrist before she could touch anything.

"Do not forget your manners, young lady. I will give you a piece." As Genny scooped a piece out for her daughter, she reminded herself to get control of her body's reactions. It wouldn't do well to have her continually fantasizing about her employee.

He was off-limits and that was that. Too bad her body wouldn't comply.

Lee lingered over the coffee, enjoying the sight of Genevieve cleaning up after supper. Her movements were jerky and ungraceful, completely unlike the woman he'd come to know that day. Something was bothering her, and he wondered if it was the same thing bothering him.

It had been a long time since Lee had been with a woman. Truthfully it had been him and his right hand for more than two years. Being around her, hearing that voice slide up and down his skin, made him hornier than he'd been in a long time.

He really had no business lusting after his boss, even if she was hands down made for loving.

Loving? He meant made for fucking—loving was the wrong damn word. Something about her made him forget everything when she opened her mouth. He'd imagine her kneeling in front of him, that mouth licking and sucking his dick, then bam! The tent was pitched in his trousers.

That was just the start of it, of course. She had a curvy body, even if she was short. Those tits, holy Christ, they were the perfect size for his hand. He couldn't help but notice her nipples harden during dinner. After that, he had trouble swallowing his food when all he could think about was what color those nipples were. Perhaps they were light pink like her lips, or a darker rose like a flower. Lee shifted uncomfortably in the chair. At this rate, he'd never be able to stand up again. When she set the last plate on the shelf above the sink, she turned and put her hands on her hips, frowning.

"I hate to ask, but I'm thinking Sophie needs a bath and so do I. Do you mind hauling the tub in here from behind the house?"

Oh hell, now he could imagine what she looked like naked in the bath. God sure had a shitty sense of humor.

"Mr. Blackwood?" She stepped toward him. "Lee?"

His name on her lips sent a pulse through him, leaving a trail of tingles as it went. "Sure. I'll go get it for you." As he stood, he recognized there was no hope for it, he'd have to let her see exactly what she did to him.

However, God must've taken pity on him because she turned to stoke up the fire in the stove and reached for the metal buckets on the floor, giving him the chance to turn his back and walk toward the door. Unfortunately, she was right behind him heading for the well.

He stopped and took the buckets from her. "I'll get the water first so you can start heating it, then I'll bring in the tub."

As she stammered a thank you, he escaped into the cool night, buckets clanking in his hand while his body throbbed.

Lee wasn't one to go around peeping at women. It wasn't something he would have ever done, apparently until he met Genevieve Blanchard. Right about then, he was a man who scented a woman and followed his dick to the small window near the kitchen sink.

He'd been the one to fetch the buckets of water for her and drag the tub into the kitchen from its perch on the porch. Dammit he knew she was going to bathe and should have been the gentleman who stayed in the barn doing chores until she was finished, or at least until she called him. However, Lee had stopped pretending to be a gentleman years earlier.

After arguing with himself for another forty-five seconds, he gave in to the raging hunger inside him and looked in the window.

Sweet Mother of God.

Every muscle in his body tensed all at once. His breath came in small bursts, low and rough as it edged out of his mouth into the blackness of the night. Blood rushed through his veins, whooshing past his ears as his heart pounded so hard he swore it cracked a rib.

She stepped out of her dress and stood in only her chemise. The lamp behind her illuminated her to the point where she didn't even need a chemise because she was naked as far as Lee was concerned. Sweet luscious curves abounded, revealed inch by inch as she pulled off the cotton garment. As he drank in Genevieve completely nude, he promptly forgot to breathe.

She was exquisite.

Her long brown hair glowed like a copper sunset in the light from the fire. It hung in waves down her back, caressing the top of the most beautiful ass he'd ever seen. Round, perfect globes, pale and plump. She wasn't thin or bony, but blessed with a body a man could hold onto while he plunged in.

His head swam with images of Genevieve beneath him, above him and beside him, and best of all, kneeling in front of him. Lightheaded and sweating, Lee hung onto the windowsill as if it were a lifeline. It seemed that every drop of blood in his body had rushed to his dick, which was now hard enough to actually hammer a nail. It throbbed in his britches, pushing against the fabric and begging for release.

She turned to step into the tub and Lee was able to see her breasts. Her skin was like honey, warm and sweet, with nipples peaked in the cool air. They were puckered as if waiting for his mouth, his tongue, his teeth. A tiny moan burst from his throat and he had to duck to swallow the howl that rose from his center.

The tall grass around him scratched at his pants as Lee clenched his jaw shut and tried to calm his arousal. He had never been so horny in his life, even with Fiona. With her he'd been eager and needy, but it was nothing compared to what he felt now.

Even just looking at Genevieve nude, without touching her, had sent him into a spiral of pure lust that would likely last for hours. He knew his hard-on would.

When the window above him opened, Lee held his breath intentionally this time. He was lucky he had squatted onto the ground below the window. Now all he could do was pray she didn't look down.

"Hello? Is anyone there?"

The smell of female wafted over him, a combination of roses, the sweetness of sugar in tea and delicate perspiration. It shouldn't have any effect on Lee, but it did anyway. He wanted to lick her skin, absorb her into his body and savor the taste of Genevieve on his tongue. Scrambling to control his breathing, his heart and his stupidity, Lee pressed his fist against his forehead. She mustn't know he was there, drinking his fill of her without her knowledge like a common bastard.

When the window closed, seemingly an hour later, Lee let out a small shaky breath and stayed put. No need to move just yet and he might hurt himself if he did. The achingly hard piece of wood between his legs was wedged in his drawers and twisted in the fabric a bit now. If he stood too quickly, there could be damage.

What the hell was he going to do now? Apparently let his dick control his actions.

Against his better judgment, he stood to peep in the window again. Genevieve was just getting into the water, surrounded by wisps of steam rising from the heated bath. He could only stare helplessly as she disappeared into the tub. To his delight, her breasts remained above the water, bobbing gently. The nipples were a deep rose color, and the sight of them in the dim firelight made him lick his lips.

His hand drifted to his trousers and unbuttoned them, freeing his constrained erection. He let out a small sigh as his hand closed around the throbbing hardness. What he wouldn't give to have her hand circling his dick instead of his own. As he stroked and squeezed his hardness, he watched her bathe. With each swipe of the cloth against her wet skin, he tugged at his own.

It was wrong and he knew it, but there was no way in hell he could stop. Not now. He pinched the base of his dick as he grew closer to coming.

Splash, moan, splash, grunt.

Like a secret ballet, his calloused hand slid up and down his sweat-soaked dick matching her movements in the water. Just as his balls tightened and his orgasm swept over him, she stood, water sluicing down her body. He slid into a crouch and came into the dirt beneath him, biting back the howl that threatened to explode from his throat as the pleasure coursed through him.

God he wanted to fuck her, to lick her, taste her. He wanted her.

As the pulses of pleasure receded, he managed to suck in a breath and tried to focus on what he'd just done without wincing in embarrassment. Genevieve was going to drive him mad, that was a certainty. If he kept on behaving like a horny teenage boy, he'd be getting himself off several times a day.

With heated cheeks, he kicked dirt over the evidence of his self-pleasuring and crept away into the dark to fasten his pants.

As she dried herself, Genny resisted the urge to linger over her painfully hard nipples. After hearing the noise outside, she had the silly fantasy that Lee had been observing her bathe. She even took extra time getting undressed to prolong the game for herself. The foolish thing was, she wanted him to actually be there. Her body still throbbed with the hum of arousal from watching him, fantasizing about him.

Playing sexual games really wasn't like her, and that's what bothered her the most. There weren't many things throughout her life that were under her control, but one of them had always been her physical reactions, particularly to men. Henry was a shitty lover, selfish and clumsy. Genny hadn't gotten a single moment of pleasure from having sex with her husband at all. It

66

was like one of her farm chores, boring but necessary. Her experience before Henry had been horrific, the stuff of nightmares she still experienced now and again.

She shook her head to dislodge the dark feelings that always overtook her when she started thinking about Camille. She'd promised herself when she moved to Tanger that she'd stop thinking about her life before Texas, the squalor she'd been used to, and the disregard for human beings she witnessed daily as a child. Nothing about the farm reminded her of the dark street in New Orleans so there was no need to dwell on it.

No, she'd much rather remember why she'd been aroused in the bathtub in the first place. Truthfully, she had never experienced pleasure with a man, only by her own hand.

Right now though, she ached for release. One day with Lee and she was fantasizing about being intimate with him, without even a smidge of interest from him. He grunted, answered in one syllable or ignored her. There was no rhyme or reason to her body's apparent infatuation with the man. It should set off warning bells inside her.

Genny couldn't risk being distracted by a man when she needed to focus on getting the wheat crop in. Too much depended on her keeping her mind and her body on that task and not on Lee Blackwood. She knew her options with men were limited, even if widows had the freedom to choose a bed partner. Until the blond one-armed man had swaggered into her life, there hadn't been a man she would choose.

As an intelligent, strong woman with needs, sometimes she just had to let herself feel. And at that moment, she was feeling quite a bit. As the towel rubbed across her skin, it pebbled up, sending shivers through her. God how she wished it was a calloused hand instead of the rough material. She could look for him, but knew it wasn't a good idea even if her mind raced with the possibility of what would happen if she found him. What would happen if he was just as willing as she was.

A shiver wracked her body at the thought. No matter how much she wanted to, it just wasn't a good idea, and that was that. With something like remorse, she picked up her nightdress to put it on. A small knock at the door had her jumping out of her skin.

Heart pounding, she had to swallow before she answered. She knew who it was, yet she called out anyway. "Who is it?"

There was a pause. "It's Lee Blackwood. I, uh, wondered if you were done with the tub. I can empty it and take it out for you."

He sounded strange, almost talkative, and she hadn't yet heard him speak so fast either. Perhaps her fantasy wasn't hers alone. Tingles raced through her at the thought and a single heavy throb resounded in her lower belly.

"Not yet. About five more minutes."

The sound of boots scraping on the wooden porch sounded outside the door. "Well, okay. I'll just sit a spell out here and wait then."

Her pulse pounded through her veins as she stared at the door, knowing he stood on the other side. All she had to do was open it and ask him in, her nude body the only invitation required. Dampness coated her pussy as she trembled with a nearly overwhelming arousal. She needed him quite badly at the moment.

What would be the harm? She was a widow and he wasn't married—a perfectly acceptable arrangement done all the time, discreetly of course. Folks in town, including Hettie and her posse, had to know Lee was there with her alone. They'd never openly shunned her, but they also never opened their arms to Genny or Sophie. Part of that was because Henry had been such an ass he put people off. However, part of it was the fact Genny appeared one day at his side, wide-eyed and angry with a wedding band on her finger. She had not been exactly friendly to the people in Tanger that first year, and she was sure they had long memories.

So why should she care if they knew Lee was at the farm? Gabby must've told the townsfolk about her need for a farmhand, and everyone knew Henry had passed on. After all, he died at Aphrodite's saloon with a beer in one hand and a whore's tit in the other. No one would blame Genny for turning to another man for solace in her bed.

Her nipples ached to be touched and her body craved a release, one that didn't involve her hand. Growing up, she had been witness to the ways men and women could be together, and many of them were still crystal clear in Genny's memory. She wanted to try them with Lee, even if it meant she was a loose woman, because she sure as hell wasn't a whore. No money was changing hands between them, simply work and trade for goods.

She wanted him, that was for certain. The question was, how much? Water puddled on the floor around her feet as she stood there, heart thumping like mad, and continued to stare at the door. Genny knew she wasn't pretty but she'd been told her raspy voice was nice by several men. Her breasts were large and she was curvy, if not particularly tall. If she offered herself to Lee, he might say no. Was she willing to take that risk?

Genny stepped toward the door and reached for the knob.

Lee stood on the corner of the porch and stared up at the night sky. Stars winked in the velvety blackness, reminding him of just how different things were in Texas than Georgia. Even the sky looked different. He sometimes wished so hard life was like it had been before the war. It was an ache deep in his chest that could bring tears to his eyes.

He scratched at the stump of his arm and recognized the stark reminder that life would never be the way it was, no matter how hard he might wish for it. God couldn't give back an arm, and he sure as hell couldn't make life from the ashes of Lee's soul.

The door to the house opened and he turned, expecting Genevieve to wave him inside for the tub. His melancholy meanderings must've made him slower than molasses because he had to blink twice before he realized that she was only wearing a towel.

Holy shit.

His arousal, partially sated by his own hand, roared to life like a locomotive. He stood frozen in place, unsure of exactly what he should do. She saved him the trouble of deciding when she turned to look at him.

The first thing he noticed was she was flushed, and he wasn't sure if it was entirely from the hot water. The second thing was, her mouth was slightly open as if she was breathing hard. His heart slammed against his rib cage and he swallowed hard.

"Miz Blanchard?" he managed to croak.

"Genny please, call me Genny." She fiddled with the towel under her arm, but she kept her focus on him. "Do you want to come inside now?"

Jesus, please us, that was a question with a hundred meanings. Lee's body, however, knew what meaning he wanted it to be.

Genny.

Yes, that fit her better than Genevieve, a mouthful of

French name he had trouble wrapping his tongue around. No doubt he'd have no trouble with her breasts though. They strained against the towel, the nipples obviously hard beneath the material.

"Mr. Blackwood?" She cleared her throat. "Lee?"

Without a sound, he strode toward her and she backed into the house. By the time she was through the doorway, he was right in front of her, his body more than ready. After he closed the door behind him, he wasn't sure what to do next, until she dropped the towel and he dropped to his knees.

Her breasts were beautiful up close, the dark pink nipples tight and begging for attention. He cupped the left one, the weight perfect in his palm, and swept his thumb across the turgid peak. She hissed in a breath, which became a strangled moan when his mouth closed around the right.

"God, yes." Her whispered exclamation let Lee know he was doing it right.

He laved the nipple, then skimmed it across his bottom teeth, before he gently bit it. She trembled at his touch, and a sheen of perspiration broke out across her beautiful skin. As he sucked the nipple deep into his mouth and tugged, her knees almost gave way. She stopped herself by grabbing his shoulders.

"Bedroom."

He didn't need to know which one. No doubt the brat was sleeping in her own room, which left Genny's room. He hoped the door had a lock because he planned on being naked with her for a few hours and didn't want any interruptions.

When Lee scooped her up with his right arm, she let out a short squeak but quickly wrapped her legs around him, pressing her damp cunt into his belly. He could feel the heat through the fabric and could think of no other moisture he wanted christening his shirt. Her breasts pressed into his chest, the nipples reminding him they were still in need of attention.

"Lee." She breathed his name and he looked up at her. Her pupils were wide with arousal and her cheeks were still flushed. Genny wasn't plain at all—he'd been completely wrong about that. She was stunningly beautiful with her wide mouth and cinnamon-kissed freckles, and her expressive brown eyes told him everything he needed to know.

She'd been hurt, probably physically and emotionally, and still she was so damn strong. Yet it seemed as though she needed him just as much as he needed her. Genny was more like him than he even imagined.

Lee stepped through the door to his room, and she gently closed it behind him. He set her on her feet, and the feel of her body sliding against his made him groan with anticipation, particularly when her heat touched his throbbing dick through his trousers. God, he didn't remember being so aroused with Fiona. With her it had been more of a frantic fucking in the alley or in a dark corner of a tent, since she always had only five minutes for him.

Lee glanced behind him and with a satisfaction he didn't expect, he turned the key in the lock above the doorknob. It was time.

His body had never been so hard, or so ready, not that he'd been overly experienced at sex. Deep down at an elemental level though, he knew this was different, very different, and he welcomed it because it made him feel. He hadn't felt much but darkness and fury for too long. Genny's magic wound its way around him, drawing him into her arms, into the lightness of her soul.

Words didn't seem necessary.

She undressed him slowly and he let her. What he wanted

to do was throw her on the bed and fuck her until neither one of them could see straight. Yet he didn't because he craved this, whatever it was, and his own rash actions were never to be trusted. So he let her lead and show him what she desired, although he shook with the need to act.

With each button she opened, Genny kissed the exposed skin. Her lips were soft and warm, almost hot, and occasionally her tongue would reach out and lap at him. Lee couldn't stop a small moan from escaping the first time she did it. He hadn't had a woman pleasure him like that before.

She pulled the shirt from his trousers and slid it off, then she pressed her breasts into his bare chest. He closed his eyes, almost coming in his drawers at the sensation of skin on skin. It was pitiful to think he hadn't actually ever been nude with a woman before, not that there were more than a handful, but they had been whores without time for this kind of mutual pleasuring or even to take all their clothes off.

Genny was a lady, a widow who needed him as much as he needed her. This was no pity fuck, no money changing hands. It was a mutual joining of bodies and he could hardly stand the wait, but he did because she wanted him to.

She ran her hands across his chest, lightly scratching at his nipples. The sensation shot straight down his belly to his balls, which were tighter than a pair of walnuts at that moment. She leaned forward and licked his flat nipples, followed by a bite for each one in turn.

He loved it.

Then she touched his shoulders and his arms. He held his breath, waiting for her to be revolted by the scarred remains of his left arm, but she continued touching him, and he could breathe again.

"You are a beautiful man, Lee Blackwood."

Before he could respond to that ridiculous notion, she pulled his head down and kissed him. Oh, sweet heavenly saints, her lips were even better against his own. Soft and warm, pliable and firm, she kissed as if she knew exactly what he needed, what he wanted, what he craved.

Her breath mixed with his as their mouths opened, tongues dueled and the temperature in the room rose exponentially. Sweet, hot wet kisses that melded them together until he couldn't tell where his mouth ended and hers began. Their tongues rasped in unison as he pressed his hardness into her softness and her arms wrapped around his neck, drawing him closer to her.

They kissed for what seemed like hours and Lee was surprised to find he wasn't as impatient as he had been. As if the kissing were as sexually satisfying as plunging into her, or at least pleasurable enough that he wanted to kiss her all night. It was all mixed up in his head, but he did know that Genny fit him as well as the key in the lock behind him. He wouldn't have believed it if she wasn't standing there kissing him, her naked and him half-naked with a dick harder than a steel bar.

When her hands landed on his trousers, his erection jumped at her. She chuckled under her breath, the husky sound making his breathing even more ragged. Genny continued to kiss him, even as she freed him, thereby allowing the constriction to be released. He could hardly remember a time he'd been so glad to have his drawers pulled down.

Then she wrapped her hand around him and Lee forgot everything but her touch. Her small hand was strong with light calluses, and when she fondled him up and down, he couldn't stop the groan bursting from his throat. She swallowed it and sucked at his tongue, even as her nimble fingers showed him how a hand should stroke an erection.

"I need..." he managed to croak. "Genny, I-I can't..." He was so close to coming, embarrassment made his cheeks heat.

She seemed to understand and lightened her touch, then tweaked the head of his dick before pulling her hands away. He wanted to cry at the loss, but then she pushed his trousers down and her cheek brushed against his bereft member. It proceeded to smack her in the eye for her trouble.

"Jesus Christ, I'm sorry." Lee couldn't have been more surprised when he saw her laughing instead of being angry.

What other woman would find it funny that the man's cock she was just handling punched her in the eye? How did he end up with such a woman? Not to question a gift, he stepped out of his trousers and waited for her to stand.

As she did, she reached out and licked the length of him, pausing to suck the head into the hot recess of her mouth. Lee's knees nearly gave out.

"You do that again and we'll be done way too soon." His voice sounded harsher than he intended, but Genny just smiled at him, gave him one more suck then cupped his balls and squeezed gently.

When she was standing in front of him again, he marveled at how playful and sexy she was. Beneath the plain, farm-wife exterior beat the heart of a lioness, a woman who knew what she wanted and took it. Lee found that the thought of a coy, meek woman held no appeal whatsoever.

His pulse throbbed through him, making it difficult to hear or think. She took his hand and led him to the bed, giving him a quick hard kiss before she climbed in and lay down. Lee stood there, staring, harder and more aroused than he'd ever been in his life. When she crooked her finger, he followed and lay on top of her. Genny opened her legs and he slid into her. The tight, wet heat surrounded him, making his heart simply stop.

There were few moments in his life he could remember with crystal-clear details. This would be one of the moments, he knew it as well as he knew this would not be the last time they shared a bed. She fit him perfectly in more ways than one. Why hadn't he seen it before? Anger made him reckless and stupid, and apparently blind as well.

She grasped his buttocks and pulled. "Ride me, cowboy."

Lee captured her lips in a bruising kiss as he let instinct take over. Genny was no loose woman, in fact she was tighter than a fist, pulsing around him as he plunged into her. She lifted her legs and wrapped them around his hips, drawing him deeper into her cunt. As he thrust, she pushed up and tilted herself, creating a rhythm as old as time.

He wrenched his mouth away and drew in a shaky breath, looking down into the face of the woman who had turned him inside out in under fifteen minutes. Her eyes were wide, her mouth open and her expression one of sweet pleasure. He found himself smiling and squelching the urge to howl at the moon like a coyote.

"Now, Lee, please, now." She scratched at his back and arched up.

Lee latched onto her breast and fucked her faster, harder. Tingles radiated out from his balls, signaling his release was imminent. He bit down on her nipple and she tightened around him so much, he came instantly. Stars exploded behind his eyes as the orgasm rippled through him. Vaguely he heard her whisper his name, keeping as quiet as possible, even as pleasure washed over them, leaving them breathless and spent.

With one last lick he let her nipple go and slid off her, settling beside her on the bed as if he belonged there. His body still pulsed with the force of the little death he'd just experienced, one more powerful than he'd known existed. As soon as he got his breath back, he propped himself up with his right hand and looked at her.

She focused on the ceiling, her nipples as hard as diamonds, her skin covered with a sheen of perspiration. The mingled scents of their bodies, the sex and the come, made the room feel like a cocoon of bliss. Lee never thought himself to be a poet, but damned if he didn't feel a poem was coming on.

"Thank you," she whispered.

He wasn't sure what to make of her remark. "Thank you too" seemed like an appropriate response even if he had no idea what she was thinking.

"I'll need to get cleaned up and check on Sophie." Genny sat up and turned to look down at him. "I'll get you some warm water to wash up with."

She was up and out of the bed, out the bedroom door, naked, before he could react. He obviously didn't need to worry about her wanting more from him than he could give. In fact, he might have to worry the opposite was true. Lee wanted this again, the heat, the sex, the rush, and now he wasn't sure she did.

As his body cooled, so did his ardor and his confidence. Genny Blanchard just knocked him off his feet, literally and figuratively. Lee stared at the door and wondered how his life had changed so quickly, and what tomorrow would bring.

Chapter Five

Genny felt like a coward when she set the pitcher of water by the door and left it there after knocking. As she entered Sophie's room, she let out a shaky breath and pressed a hand to her mouth. She wanted to cry, and she wanted to laugh. She had no idea inviting Lee to her bed would change her.

Oh, she expected to be satisfied, to have finally scratched the itch she'd been suffering from. Yet the amazing sex she just had with him went far beyond that expectation and left her trembling and a bit confused. She had to be alone with her thoughts and figure out exactly how she felt. Genny was no virgin—she had experience in bed with a man—but she hadn't expected it to be any different with Lee.

She couldn't have been more wrong.

Sophie slept in her bed with an angelic peacefulness she never had during the day. Genny's heart flipped at the sight of her daughter's innocence. Life had been quite different when the day began. Now everything was mixed up and Genny knew she was to blame.

She chose to go to town and ask for help. She chose to convince Lee to work for her. She chose to invite him to her bed. All her own choices, so why did she feel so out of control?

After setting the second pitcher of water on the washstand, she washed off the remnants of the sex as quietly and quickly as possible. The cool night air made her skin pebble even as the warm water soothed her tender parts. As she pulled on her nightdress, it felt heavy and scratchy on her tender skin, but she put it on just the same. She climbed into bed next to Sophie without disturbing the girl.

As she stared up at the ceiling, Genny's mind refused to turn off. It replayed each and every second of what she'd just shared with Lee with startling clarity. She knew she should have simply gotten dressed before she opened the door. Instead, she threw caution to the wind and complicated things by having incredible, indescribable, unforgettable sex with her employee.

She couldn't regret the mutual pleasure they'd found, not for a moment. Genny decided he'd been as surprised as she by the way things had turned out. For her, she'd expected some satisfying sex, but surely not the emotional surge she experienced at his touch.

Genny lay in bed wide awake long into the night. The morning would be awkward enough, facing Lee again after being intimate with him, but she'd do it with little-to-no rest. However, she couldn't make sleep come, no matter how gritty her eyes were, or how many times she yawned. A little voice inside her piped up with the truth Genny didn't want to acknowledge—she would have slept soundly if she had stayed with Lee.

The sun seemed to rise earlier than normal, shining into Genny's grainy eyes. Her feet dragged like anchors as she mechanically made coffee, splashing cold water on her dress when she tried to settle the grounds.

"Damn." She wiped at the water with a rag, wondering if she would ever feel awake that day.

"Good morning." Lee's voice sent a shiver through her from head to toe.

"My hands hurt," Sophie piped up from the table where she sat munching on her biscuit. "I don't like working in the barn."

"It's no fun for me either, brat." The sound of a chair scraping told her Lee sat down. "But chores is chores and they need to be done."

Genny wrapped a rag around the handle of the coffee pot and picked it up from the stove. When she turned to glance at him, he looked even more sinfully handsome than he had the day before. His blond hair was slightly too long and had started to curl up around his ears. She twitched with the urge to run her fingers through the wheat-colored waves.

Well, certainly the attraction hadn't faded a whit, in fact it appeared to be stronger. Lee, however, wasn't looking at her at all. He sat at the table and seemed to be very interested in his fingernails as she poured the coffee. She wasn't sure if she should be insulted or not.

"I've got the harness nearly ready. I need you to try it on so I can make sure the size is right." She set the coffee pot back on the stove and fixed a plate of bacon, biscuits and eggs for him. No doubt he had a big appetite after such strenuous activities.

The thought made her want to laugh, but she swallowed the urge back down. No need for him to think she was as crazy as her mind was that morning.

"Sure thing, Miz Blanchard. I appreciate you working on it."

Miz Blanchard? Now she really was insulted. The man had had various parts of his body intertwined and melded with hers—there was no call to use her formal name like that. He was being ornery on purpose.

"I'd do it for anyone in need really." Genny fixed her own plate while gritting her teeth. "It's the Christian thing to do after all. Helping souls in need, I mean."

When her plate hit the table, his head snapped up and he

finally looked at her. What she'd taken for rudeness and dismissal was actually fear and doubt. That changed things and let the wind out of her sails of righteous anger.

"It's especially nice to be able to help someone I know and, uh, like." She offered him a small smile, and he nodded before turning back to his food.

"Well I don't like him." Sophie spoke around the half-eaten biscuit in her mouth. "He's bossy."

Genny swallowed a scalding mouthful of coffee so she didn't choke on it. "That's not very polite, and Mr. Blackwood here is only telling you to do your chores. Why, I'd do the same thing if I was in the barn, and you know it."

Sophie furrowed her brow and looked at her mother. "Your face is all red and there's a rash on your neck, Mama. You ain't getting sick, are you?"

Oh, hell and damnation. Genny hadn't counted on whisker burn, but given her pale skin, it would be inevitable there'd be evidence left. "No, I was hot last night and scratched myself up a bit. It's nothing." Her eyes flickered to Lee's for just a moment and that's all it took for her arousal to spark. His nostrils flared and her pussy throbbed. Well, she had her answer as to whether or not they both wanted it again.

"Why don't you work on brushing Ned this morning? I'll bet he'd enjoy that." Genny continued as if she wasn't flushed and stupidly horny. "He did a lot of work yesterday and needs some special attention."

Sophie stood and narrowed her eyes. "I'll take care of *our* horse in *our* barn. Just so long as I don't have to take no orders from the likes of *him*."

With that she walked out, nose in the air, her self-righteous crown firmly positioned on her little head. It wasn't until the door closed that a laugh burst from Genny.

"That child has entirely too much attitude," Lee grumbled. "Someone ought to take a switch to that little fanny."

Genny shook her head. "It isn't as if she doesn't come by it honest. I'm afraid I always had a bit of sass in me as well. She's just feeling...free, and giving her limits right now, well, it'd be very hard for me to do."

"I'll do it." He gulped the rest of his coffee.

"I'm sure you would." Genny smiled at his orneriness, which he apparently didn't realize mimicked Sophie's.

Lee glanced up at her. "You just going to let her run wild then?"

"It's not your business, but no, I'm not. Doing chores will help her get her own control back."

"She's seven, not twenty-seven. She needs a mother." He stood and stared at Genny with annoyance.

Genny stood and walked over to him, her anger stirred up now. "My daughter is my business, Mr. Blackwood. I'll thank you to keep your opinions to yourself on how to raise her."

He leaned down, his brown eyes dancing with indignation and passion. "You'd best start raising her right then."

"You're a bastard." Her breath came in short gasps as she tried to sort out the difference between her anger and her arousal.

"No, but I can be a son of a bitch." He grabbed her and yanked her flush against his hard body. When his lips came down on hers, they weren't gentle at all.

Damn if she didn't almost burn into a cinder right then and there. She wrapped her arms around him and scratched at his back, even as her tongue dueled with his. They might have continued on to the bedroom if Sophie hadn't stomped back in the door.

"Mama, what in tarnation are you doing kissing him?"

Genny wanted a hole to open up in the floor and swallow her right then and there. Of course, it didn't happen so she had to extricate herself from Lee and step away. With a shaky smile, she turned to her daughter.

"I was just saying thanks for all his hard work."

Sophie narrowed her eyes. "That's an awful big thank you. You don't kiss Mr. Marchison like that when he loads the wagon."

Genny managed a small chuckle even if her heart was beating so hard it actually hurt. "Mr. Marchison doesn't work for me. I pay him to load the wagon, yes, but he's not the kissing type. I just tell him thank you instead."

She heard Lee muffle a snort behind her and wanted to kick him. This was harder for her than him and he had no call to make her feel even worse. Sophie didn't look convinced at all as she marched over and sat at the table, leveling her stare at Lee.

"Ah, now let's get that harness fitted so we can get you to work." Genny forced a brightness in her tone she surely wasn't feeling. Although her body throbbed and pulsed for more, she had to force her desire away and focus on fitting the harness correctly.

Awkward wasn't quite the right word for how she felt holding the contraption up against Lee and touching him. Particularly with Sophie a foot away watching them.

Genny was more self-conscious than anything. Oh hell, she didn't know what she felt. All she knew is this man and she had a connection. Something she wouldn't have been able to explain if asked, but there was definitely something between them.

It didn't matter that he only had one arm. It didn't matter that she was a widow with a less-than-perfect past. It was

83

apparent he had been through quite a bit in his life, perhaps even as much as she had. The war had not been kind to him, that was obvious, but there was something else, something deeper. Something that had festered inside him longer than the past six or seven years.

No one got to be an adult with such a deep scar inside, even more painful than the one on the outside, without there being some kind of tragedy in his life. She was curious, but honestly, she shouldn't be poking her nose into Lee's business. It was, after all, his business.

He smelled good as if he'd just washed with soap and warm water. He'd shaved too. There was a nick on his chin. Genny had to resist the urge to kiss it.

There it was. That attraction, that indefinable link between them. She had to make a choice to either let go of her doubts and fly with it or stop the relationship completely. Genny wondered if she had wings.

"So how is this contraption supposed to work now?" Lee interrupted her musings.

"Well, um, you hook this here like this." She stuck a couple pins in her mouth to pull the sleeve up and around so she could fasten the harness on his shoulder. "Buckle it here and then on the end here I hooked something so you could use the end of it as you would a tool. I'm not sure if this is exactly the right thing to use."

She'd found a long nail amongst Henry's tools and used a hammer to pound it against the anvil until it was a hook shape. "We may find something else that might fit or work better. This kind of thing is new for me too so we'll have to figure it out as we go along. I think this will at least give us a start."

He looked at it dubiously. "Okay, if you say so. I'll give it a try."

After she made sure that her measurements were correct, she unbuckled the harness and took it off. "Give me five minutes and it should be ready for you to use."

"Okay."

"There's more coffee on the stove if you'd like some."

"I would."

Before she could offer to get him a cup, he'd done it himself. He was standing by the stove watching her as he sipped the hot brew. Sophie sat on the chair beside her, watching him, looking for all the world as if she were a miniature guard dog. She wasn't sure what it was that had gone on yesterday between Lee and Sophie, but whatever it was, he obviously hadn't succumbed to Sophie's whining, complaining or bossiness.

Genny could only think that was a good thing. After all, she admonished herself over and over for not exercising more discipline where her daughter was concerned. Lee was a stranger but he had the perspective that she didn't, and Genny was wise enough to recognize that, even if she wasn't smart enough to do something about it herself.

"Why is he staring at us, Mama?"

"Sophie, Mr. Blackwood is waiting for me to finish this harness so he can finish cleaning up the barn. To finish what you started yesterday."

"I ain't working in the barn today, especially with him. I already said that."

"You mind your manners, Miss Sophie Marie Blanchard. Mr. Blackwood deserves your respect and so do I. If you don't want to give it to us, then I will paddle your behind and put you in the corner for the rest of the day where you can think about how hard it is to be polite and respectful."

Genny surprised herself with her stern words. It was the first glimmer of being a parent, of being the parent she should be to her daughter. Sophie seemed to be as shocked as Genny.

"Uh, well, okay." Sophie sounded quiet and unsure of herself.

Genny wondered if she'd gone too far. She glanced up at Lee and noted the approval in his expression. It wasn't his business, but just the same, he noticed Sophie's wildness right off as most folks did. Genny winced inwardly knowing that Lee's first day had been spent with a house full of mad females and even crazier shenanigans, not to mention knee-deep in horse shit.

What must he think of her? God only knew what she thought of herself. She pricked her finger three times pushing the needle through the heavy leather and canvas. As promised, within five minutes the harness was complete.

"Finished!" She held it up.

One blond brow rose. "It ain't like it's a cotillion dress."

A cotillion. A word from a million years ago that conjured up images of peeking through enormous paned-glass windows and seeing beautiful white, yellow, blue and pink dresses. Girls with grown-up hairdos and boys pulling at their ties, straightening their suit jackets as they asked the girls to dance.

Lee's deep drawl pulled her back from her thoughts. She shook her head, trying to resist the urge to get lost in the past, to remember where she was, who she was, and what was important.

"No, it surely isn't a dress. It is something that should help you, Mr. Blackwood. Now put your coffee down and get the harness finished so you can get to work."

This time when she touched him his body temperature had risen. The heat came off him, making her own body too warm.

Maybe it was the coffee or the stove, or maybe it was because she was touching him again. Her fanciful imagination seemed to want to conjure up all kinds of connections between her and Lee that didn't exist. Whether or not she wanted them didn't seem to be important.

She couldn't help but notice the small baby-fine hairs at the base of his neck. Light blond curls like silk, begging for her touch. Against her will, she skimmed them with her fingers as she reached for the last buckle.

He froze in place and she sighed. The air almost crackled between them.

Genny stepped back and ran a critical eye over her handiwork. It wasn't pretty but it fit him well and she hoped it would help him. "Well, I guess the next thing left to do is give it a try and hope it works."

Lee glanced at his left arm, flexed it, moved what was now his hand of sorts, the hook on the end. He looked back up at her, and she saw respect in his expression.

It was a gift, a small one, but a gift just the same.

"Thank you kindly, Miz Blanchard. This is a right fine thing to do."

As if a curtain fell over his true self, he blinked and all the emotion was gone. He gulped the last of his coffee, took his hat from the back of his chair, and nodded at Genny. As he walked out the door, she wondered what it would be like if he was her husband leaving to work on the farm for the day. An illusion where she could wake up with him in bed each morning and sleep beside him in bed each night. A partner instead of a boss or a master. To have someone who cared she was there, who looked forward to seeing her in the morning, to greeting her in the evening. It was another fanciful notion, but somewhere deep down buried inside the layers of cynicism and hard reality, little

Genny Boudreaux smiled at the thought.

Lee couldn't believe how well Genny's harness actually worked. It was almost like a sleeve, connected with leather straps and buckles to his shoulder. She'd fashioned a hook on the end from a long nail and given him the ability to strap his arm to the hayfork or use the nail to guide it. The difference in how much he was getting done was truly remarkable.

She was amazing and sexy enough to make him lose his mind. Thank God the brat had interrupted them or he'd have fucked her on the table. That voice, that wide mouth, that talented tongue—she was temptation incarnate and he was helpless to resist her pull.

Oh, he knew she was looking for someone to warm her bed after her husband's death, and he was a hard, willing body. Yet he couldn't help but wonder what it might be like to wake up next to her each morning.

Jesus, pretty soon he'd start acting like a lovesick calf.

"Should I be worried that you have a contraption strapped to you or not?" Zeke's voice interrupted Lee's thoughts. Thank God.

Lee swiped his sleeve across his brow and glanced up at his brother leaning against the stall door. "I'm getting twice as much done, even if I look like a damn plow horse." He held up the hook, which made the buckles jangle merrily. "Ain't it the darnedest thing? Genny made it."

Zeke's blond brows shot up toward his hairline. "Genny? Who's Genny?" Zeke peered at him with that cool stare he had pretty much perfected, the big-brother stare that had become the lawman stare. He used it on people he questioned within his jurisdiction as sheriff.

Lee immediately felt the power of that stare. Zeke always

had the ability to get the answers to questions Lee didn't really want to answer, just by leveling that powerful gaze on his little brother. The excuses Lee scrambled to find in his mind seemed stupid and ineffective. Hell, he'd been through war, death and everything in between with Zeke. They were more than brothers, if that were possible. There wasn't much they kept from each other anymore. After the war, they'd grown closer, supported each other through tough times. When Zeke had been trying to stay away from the whiskey, Lee was there for him, cleaning up vomit, piss and shit and his heart.

This situation with Genny certainly didn't compare, although Lee did feel a little like a young kid crowing about his conquest of the night before. Lee touched one of the buckles on the harness.

"Genny is Genevieve Blanchard."

"Mrs. Blanchard?" Zeke crossed his arms and leaned against the stall door, his expression expectant. "You've been here one day. How did she go from Mrs. Blanchard to Genevieve to Genny?"

Lee puffed out a breath. "Damned if I know. Can't understand why she wanted me to work here in the first place. A one-armed man isn't good for much, especially on a farm."

Zeke gestured to the harness securely fastened around Lee's arm. "Seems like she found a use for you after all."

"Yeah, that she did. Actually it was the brat's idea. Genny just made it happen."

"The brat?"

Lee sighed, knowing Zeke would continue to pepper him with questions. "If you saw this girl, or had occasion to speak to her, you'd know she's a little pain in the ass. She's got a mouth on her worse than a drunk gambler with two bits in his pocket and a whore on his lap. Brat is a much nicer word than I could

89

use."

Zeke laughed. "That's quite a picture you paint there. Does she chew tobacco and spit when she walks too?"

It did sound ridiculous. Lee felt a hint of a smile. "No, she's just a little pest, that's all, but she had a damn good idea. That lady in there has got magic fingers. I mean, uh, she can work magic with a needle."

"I noticed the new shirt. Trousers new too? Got used to seeing you in those faded grays." A look passed between them, exactly what those faded gray trousers had seen.

"Yep, she's a helluva woman, Zeke, and I think I'm in trouble." Saying it out loud made it seem that much more real.

At Lee's confession, Zeke straightened up, completely serious, the teasing wiped clean from his face. "What's happened?"

"I don't know what to make of her, Zeke. The second I laid eyes on her, heard that voice, I got all twisted up inside. I didn't know my ass from a hole in the ground. When I got here, she gave me the clothes and damn, I felt like I could do anything, like I was almost normal. And then, last night, she was taking a bath and I knocked on the door." Lee did not inform his brother of the late-night peeping at Genny as she took that bath. He had at least that amount of self-respect, or maybe it was shame. "And I thought maybe she'd want me to help her empty the tub and drag it out of the cabin. But that wasn't it at all. She came out and she was in the altogether, Zeke. And sweet Lord above, that woman is more beautiful than anything I've ever seen in my life."

Zeke leaned in closer, keeping his voice low. "What happened?"

"Somehow I got naked too and God, I ain't never, ever felt like that with a woman, Zeke." Lee trembled at the memory of the raw power of being with her. Even standing there, covered with sweat and hay, smelling of horse shit, he craved her touch, way down deep inside him. It would sit there and wait and gnaw at him until he gave in. He'd never force her, of course, but if Genny opened that door again, there was no way in hell Lee would say no.

He slid down the stable wall and sat on an upturned bucket.

"She's a widow, at least six months right?" Zeke squatted next to Lee.

"Yeah, near as I can tell her husband wasn't worth a shit either. This barn, I know you can't tell today or maybe you can, but it was in sorry shape. Moldy shit, moldy hay, they only got but one horse and that thing is older than God. The fences are falling apart, the child hasn't got a lick of discipline. This farm is held together by spit and string near as I can tell."

Zeke nodded. "Well, sounds to me like Mrs. Blanchard made a choice and you accepted. She's a widow, you're not married, ain't no reason why the two of you can't have your private pleasures in private. Nobody needs to know."

Lee let out the breath he'd been holding. He'd hoped Zeke would understand. God knew he didn't understand it. His brother's acceptance, approval maybe, was more important than just about anything. Lee had spent most of his life proving what an ass he could be, until they'd come to Texas and everything changed. Until a tiny town on the ass-edge of starvation and ruin had yanked Lee back to the land of the living and given him something worth fighting for. He'd bet every dollar he had, which wasn't much, that if they hadn't come to Tanger, he would have been dead already in a saloon brawl, maybe killed by a young buck with a shiny new gun and an attitude. Tanger had saved him just as much as he had helped save it.

Now Tanger was giving him one more gift in the form of a widow named Genny. Perhaps it was Lee's time to find someone to make him feel human again.

"Thanks, Zeke. I'm glad you came out to see me. It's, uh, mighty nice of you." It sounded awkward and stupid as usual, but the sentiment was there.

Zeke grinned and jangled the harness. "What are big brothers for? Now how about you go introduce me to your Genny?"

Lee felt like a boy bringing a girl home to meet his parents. In this case, his brother had filled the role of father for many years. Zeke's approval was more important than Lee would ever let on. He looked to his big brother for guidance even if he didn't know it.

They found her on her hands and knees in what remained of the garden. There were apparently still some vegetables left because she was pulling potatoes from the dirt. Her curvaceous ass wiggled with each yank of her hands. Lee must've stared at her for a little bit too long because Zeke nudged him with a sharp elbow.

"Miz Blanchard?" Lee thought it best to keep it formal around others as she had done with Sophie.

She answered without turning around. "I'm a little busy as you can see. Can it wait a few minutes? Or maybe Sophie can help you." *Tug, tug, yank,* oh, the fantasies he could conjure up about her hands.

"Well, no it can't." Lee sounded harsher than he intended, but damn, the woman distracted him whenever he was around her. "My brother came by."

She froze in place, her hand wrapped around a potato, hair hanging down from the kerchief she'd tied around her head.

"He's standing there beside you, isn't he? And I'm in the dirt."

"Yes, ma'am, I surely am, but I have no qualms or quarrels with a woman who is a hard worker." Zeke sounded smooth, covering up Lee's awkwardness.

With a sigh that could likely be heard round the world, Genny set the potato in the basket with the others. She clapped her hands together and rubbed to try and loosen the dirt, then stood. When she turned to face the two men, her eyes flashed fire at Lee but she just smiled at Zeke.

"It's a pleasure to meet you, Sheriff Blackwood. I'd shake your hand but I'm sure you don't want to share the last of the harvest like that."

Zeke let out a small chuckle. "Since you put it like that, no I probably wouldn't. It's a pleasure to meet you as well, Mrs. Blanchard. I remember seeing you at the Founder's Day celebration with your daughter. She's the spitting image of you."

Genny's face softened at the mention of Sophie. "Yes, she is. She nagged me for weeks to attend since we'd never gone to anything like it. Remembers your brother's shooting too."

Lee forced himself not to squirm under her stare. The girl had already told him she remembered so why should he feel embarrassed?

"He's always had a good eye and a steady hand. Best tracker in the Devils too." Zeke's praise went a long way to chasing away Lee's discomfort.

"The Devils?" Genny looked between them. "I'm not going to hell for hiring him, am I?"

If Lee didn't know any better, he would swear she winked at him. Jesus, the woman flaunted convention right and left.

He could fall in love with her so easily.

"The Devils on Horseback was the nickname of our group during the war, ma'am. We sort of used it to name our business, D.H. Enterprises, when we were looking for work after it was over." Zeke tugged at the brim of his hat. The memories of the dark months after the war when starvation rode their backs were likely prickling at his mind too.

"I don't think I have to ask why you were called that. I've heard you and your friends ride as if you were born in the saddle. So there were four of you?" Genny tried to brush the dirt off the front of her faded blue dress, but it seemed to be permanently embedded in the fabric.

"Five of us actually. One of the Devils, Nate Marchand, lives over in Grayton with his wife." Zeke smiled. "You remind me a bit of his Elisa actually."

"I assume that's a compliment. Marchand? Sounds French." Her curls began to tighten as the breeze dried the sweat on her forehead. They swayed gently, tickling her cheeks until she batted them away.

Lee noted that Zeke's gaze followed the movement. What the hell was that about? "Oh yep, it's a compliment. She's a fighter, strongest woman I've ever met. And Marchand is French. Lee used to call him Frenchie all the time." Zeke pushed at Lee's shoulder. "The two of them were like brothers who bickered constantly."

Genny's brows rose and a smile played around her lips. "I can't imagine Lee bickering with anyone."

That comment stung. "I'm not that bad."

"Oh yes you are." Zeke folded his arms and rocked back on his heels. "Nobody can be a bigger pain in the ass than you."

Then Genny shared a look with Zeke. It was an unspoken communication, one that scraped at Lee's heart like a rusty nail. "What the hell are you doing, Zeke?"

Zeke frowned. "I'm having a conversation with your Genny."

Lee's breath caught in his throat at the expression on her face. He shouldn't have told his brother anything. "She's not my Genny."

"No, I'm not, and I don't appreciate you two talking over me." Genny's brows drew together.

"I wasn't the one flirting with my brother."

Her mouth dropped open at the same time Zeke growled at him. "Lee, what the hell is wrong with you?" His brother leaned toward him. "You're acting foolish."

Old hurts opened anew and Lee was overcome with dark emotions he thought he'd left behind. "At least I'm not cheating on my wife."

"You're on dangerous ground, little brother." The air pulsed with tension as the brothers faced each other down.

"This is ridiculous. I'm not flirting, no one is cheating, and you are acting like an ass." Genny stood beside his brother.

Zeke pointed his finger. "Don't you dare bring Naomi into this. You'll regret that. I don't need to see another one of your rants, Lee. Grow up and be a man."

Lee felt it coming and was helpless to stop it. It was as if his instincts had overtaken his mind and self-preservation took precedence over common sense. "Fuck you, Zeke. Do you have to constantly make me feel as if I'm a little kid who needs a scolding? Me and Nate didn't like each other most of the time, so the hell what?" He pointed a shaking finger at a shocked-looking Genny. "And you have no call to judge me, lady, so fuck you too. Anyone with a goddamn lick of sense would clean two-month-old horse shit out of a barn."

Oh, Jesus.

Lee almost slapped his hand across his mouth, but instead he turned and walked away. To be honest, he didn't walk at all. He ran. Again.

Chapter Six

Genny didn't know who was more shocked, she or Zeke. The man bore an uncanny resemblance to Lee, but his cheeks and jaw had sharper angles, his expression was more controlled. She looked at the sheriff and watched the play of emotion on his face, from anger to pity to disappointment.

"Damn," Zeke said so softly, she barely caught it. He met her gaze with an apologetic one. "He isn't normally such an ass."

She tried to swallow but her throat had dried up, right along with her courage. She'd had no idea Lee had that much anger inside him. It had flowed out of him like a river, caustic and uncaring who it splashed on its journey.

"He's got to let that anger go." She was surprised her voice was so steady. "It's killing him."

Zeke's expression lost its controlled coolness and the aching vulnerability of a brother came through. "I know, but I can't seem to help him."

Genny decided two things. First, she liked the sheriff a lot. Anyone who looked after family, who showed love for a brother like that, was a good person, and she trusted her instincts. Second, she was going to chip away at that anger inside Lee until it exploded into a million pieces.

She took Zeke's arm. "Let's go inside and have a bit of

refreshment, Sheriff. I think we could both use some."

He looked down at her, his scrutiny probing and a bit disconcerting. After what seemed like more than enough time to evaluate her trustworthiness, he nodded.

"A refreshment sounds perfect." Zeke squeezed her hand beneath his. "My wife, Naomi, would like you."

"I think I'd like any woman brave enough to marry a Blackwood," she quipped.

Zeke threw his head back and laughed. "You are perfect for him."

Genny wanted to tell him she had no intention of keeping Lee and she wasn't perfect for him. The words never left her mouth though because she knew Zeke was right. As scary as it was, he was right.

After they settled inside, Genny felt a bit nervous, as she had when Lee first came into the cabin. The brothers were big men and the room small—they filled it with their broad shoulders and long legs. Zeke sat at the table and watched as she sliced some bread and poured water from the pitcher.

After she set the food on the table, she slid into the chair and took a deep breath. "Tell me."

Zeke didn't need further prompting. "He's been hurt so badly, I wasn't sure he would survive, and I don't just mean the wounds from the war."

"I've already seen them." Genny hadn't shied away from his physical or emotional wounds, there was no reason to. She was as damaged on the inside as he was, truth be told.

Genny wasn't sure what Zeke was going to reveal to her about Lee, but she knew the key to understanding why he was so angry was finding out what happened to him. What was it that put him on the path to self-destruction?

Zeke nibbled on his bread, staring down at the crumbs on the tin plate as if maybe they were going to tell him something. Genny was patient, Lord knew she had to be with Henry for a husband and Sophie as a daughter. If she were being honest with herself, Genny could be as difficult as Sophie at times. This, however, wasn't one of those times. She recognized that Lee was suffering, that the fury she'd heard spewing from his mouth was more than just anger. It was laced with ancient pain and new pain, and another dark emotion she couldn't quite identify.

"Lee and I," Zeke began, "we've obviously always been brothers, but it wasn't until the war and after the war that we acted like brothers. You know, we would fuss like all kids do growing up. We used to play pretend and fool around and go hunting and fishing, riding horses. See, our family back in Georgia, well, the Blackwoods, had money and lots of it. Gideon's pa was the oldest so he had the bulk of the fortune. Our pa was fifth in line so he didn't get near as much. He was the sickly one. Around the time I was twelve, Lee must've been ten, Pa came down with some kind of palsy. There was doctors, medicines and lots of things to eat up the money that we did have. Everything went toward him, and not too much went toward me and Lee except for the basics. Mama used to dote on Lee because she nearly died when he was born. There were no more young'uns after him. She babied him until he pushed her away, then when Pa grew sick, she latched onto him like he was a replacement for the children that she didn't have. It was almost like losing both parents at the same time. I did my best to be a pa to Lee, but kids are kids. We make stupid mistakes, we think we know everything, seen everything and done everything, and we ain't but spit in the wind."

The Blackwood family history was similar to stories she'd heard before, but she felt pain that Lee had endured so much at a very young age. A lump of emotion formed in her throat and she wanted to find Lee and pull him into a hug. She knew all about being disappointed and ignored by a parent. Oh, she knew it intimately well.

"As Lee got to be a teenager, he just grabbed the world by the horn and wrestled with it. Reckless, stupid teenage-boy stuff. I couldn't control him and Mama didn't even try. Pa died when Lee was fifteen so I focused on keeping the family together, keeping our house, keeping us fed, clothed and such." Zeke took a swallow of water.

Genny couldn't have been more surprised to see his hand trembling ever so slightly. The sheriff wasn't as cool as his exterior led her to believe. Why he was telling her all this, she'd figure out later.

"So, when the war started, hell Lee was barely eighteen. Gideon knew it was our duty to do what we had to do to protect the south. Jake had always been there with us. I don't know if you know Jake Sheridan. He and his wife own the mill in town."

Genny smiled. "I know Jake. Gabby is sort of a friend."

"Jake is really a Blackwood, just one of those secrets that nobody talked about. I'm fairly certain that Gideon and he share the same pa. Jake's mama stepped out on her no-account husband, leaving him to take care of a passel of sisters. We treated Jake like a brother, cousin and friend. We went to war together along with Nate." Zeke shook his head. "The war seemed to turn Lee into even more of a raging bull. He would plow right through enemy lines with guns firing right and left, and cannons exploding just missing his fool head. God knows the boy must have nine lives like a cat."

Genny thought it interesting Zeke referred to Lee as a boy when she knew firsthand he was definitely all man. Perhaps because his brother still thought of him as a boy, Lee acted like one. It was an opinion she didn't want to share with the serious sheriff yet.

"How did he lose his arm?"

"That's the dumbest thing of all. See, through all the stunts he pulled, it was his hootin' and hollerin' and that rebel yell during our midnight raids that started the whole Devils on Horseback. It would run a chill up a body's spine just to hear it in the dead of night. Through all that, he barely came away with a scratch. It was just maybe a month or six weeks before the war ended and I knew Lee had been keeping time with one of the camp women. She disappeared, picked up and left. I think maybe she knew we were on our last legs. Half of us didn't have shoes, the other half had sores or wounds, our clothes were in tatters. Like a rat, she abandoned a sinking ship."

Genny could tell whoever this camp woman was, there was no love lost between she and Zeke.

"He got drunk the day after she left, when he accepted that she wasn't coming back. After that he was like a snarling bull, with no thought for anything but killing. I was pinned down by a couple of Yankees, and Lee rode through like a screaming banshee to get me out. Son of a bitch Yankee got off a lucky shot that hit him in the arm. A million times that happened it wouldn't have gone through the bone, but it did and shattered it. Ain't no way the doc could've fixed it. He had to cut it off." He wiped his brow with his sleeve and Genny reached over to put her hand over his.

"You don't have to tell me anymore. I don't want to put you through remembering something that causes you such pain." She wasn't surprised at all that Lee risked his life to save his brother. They seemed to be devoted to each other, a deep bond that went beyond blood, because Genny knew that wasn't always strong.

101

Zeke looked up at her, evaluating her or maybe judging her. She didn't know which or why. Then he spoke again. "You know, Lee isn't what you'd call experienced with ladies. He's kind of a babe in the woods and when he told me about last night—pardon me, but we share just about anything, not telling tales or anything, he just needed to talk—I was afraid you were going to be like Fiona, taking that boy for what he can give you. From what I can tell, Miss Genny, you are someone he could love, really love. I didn't believe in love myself until I met my Naomi. Sometimes God has a plan for us that we're not privy to, but it's laid out there in front of us to follow. Don't use him, don't hurt him, love him and respect him. That's all I ask of you."

Genny sat back, completely flummoxed by Zeke. Lee had already told his brother what had happened the night before? She hadn't even come to grips with it herself. Her insides were all topsy-turvy. Actually she was a little jealous of Lee having someone to talk to about what happened. Genny didn't have anybody to talk to.

She took Zeke's words and mulled over them for a few minutes, wondering if she should feel embarrassed. "He's a good man, that brother of yours. He's not a lost boy, but a man who's been hurt. I don't know about the love part yet, but the respect part is easy. I already do respect him. I don't plan on hurting him and I surely won't use him." What she didn't tell him was that she was already a little bit in love. She liked having Lee there, liked being with him even if he was a bit ornery, and certainly the man had a temper. She was no prize herself, but she believed Zeke was right about the path. It was laid out in front of her. If she looked to her right, she just might see Lee right there next to her. She could only hope that the love would come with time.

Right there she made a decision that she would open

herself up to Lee. She had nothing to lose and so much to gain.

Lee sat under a big tree at the edge of the wheat field, pulling up weeds and tossing them into the breeze. He'd acted like such a complete bastard to Genny. Zeke would get over it; he was used to Lee's temper. But Genny, God, he'd actually said "Fuck you" to her. What the hell was he thinking?

He hadn't been thinking at all, that was the problem. Once again, he'd let his temper rule him. What a complete fool. He wanted to control his outbursts, had thought perhaps being away from Tanger would help. Instead, he had found himself falling in love with a widow who pulled emotions out of him by the handful.

Jesus, did he deserve any woman? No chance he could possibly explain why he acted like that when he didn't even understand it. He'd have to apologize. Something he really, really hated doing. Not only was it like yanking teeth, but he felt about two inches tall when he did it.

"So this is where you're hiding."

Genny's voice startled him so much he smacked his head into the trunk of the tree.

"I'm not hiding."

"You should be." She sat down cross-legged on the ground and started pulling up weeds too. "That was not good, Lee. Really not good."

He didn't say anything, couldn't because his throat had closed up, so he nodded.

"Your brother went back to town. He said he'd see you soon and expected an apology when he did." She leaned back against the side of the tree so they were shoulder to shoulder. "I know he probably wouldn't admit it, but I think you hurt his feelings."

This was not what Lee wanted to hear. He knew he had said some nasty things, but enough to hurt the steel-skinned Zeke? Not likely, or maybe he was just denying how much he had done.

They sat in silence for a few minutes while Lee digested the plate of shit she'd brought for him to eat. He deserved every bit of it too.

"I don't know why I said those things." His voice was a whisper on the wind.

"I do. You don't want to hope for anything, to wish anything good will happen. If it doesn't, you don't get hurt." Her insight was uncanny and it unnerved him a bit.

"Why would you think that?"

Her laugh was strained, barely audible. "Because you're just like me."

That made him turn to look at her for the first time since she'd sat next to him. Her expression was full of sadness, understanding and even a bit of wistfulness.

"I've spent my life not hoping for anything and I haven't been disappointed. Until I had Sophie, there was nothing in my life worth fighting for or the pain of loving." She cupped his cheek. "You've had a hard path in life, Lee."

This time he couldn't speak because he swallowed the tears that threatened. She had seen right through his wall, his self-defenses, into his dark heart.

"I can't be more than I am," he managed to choke out. "I'm half a man, Genny. For God's sake, I just treated you like shit."

"Then apologize."

"That's it? All I have to do is apologize?" He stared at her, disbelieving his stupidity would be forgiven so easily.

"No, you have to make it up to me every day for a very long

time, but an apology is a good start." She kissed him softly. "So what will you do?"

He pressed his forehead against hers. "I'm sorry, Genny, so sorry for what I said, what I did."

She nodded. "Good. Now let's get back to the farm. You've got work to do."

Lee kissed her hard. "Lead the way, boss lady."

They walked back to the farm side by side, not touching, but he felt the connection nonetheless. He wasn't sure what had happened after he stormed off, perhaps Zeke had told her some things. Whatever it was, he had another opportunity with his Genny and for that, he was grateful. Maybe even hopeful.

Two days after Zeke visited, Lee was shaving in his temporary bedroom when he spotted a ledger book beneath the bed. Numbers had become something he did well even if he'd taken some time off to work at the farm. He really shouldn't be concerned with it, but his gaze kept returning to the book as he finished getting dressed.

When he looked down at his boots, the ledger was right between them on the floor. One peek couldn't hurt, right? He picked it up and sat on the bed, ready to do some reading.

Twenty minutes later, he walked into the kitchen and knew he was scowling. What the hell kind of idiot was Henry Blanchard? The fool could not have made a bigger mess of the accounts for the farm. Not only was his handwriting terrible, but it seemed he took out money he never recorded. The credits and debits added up to crazy numbers that didn't make a lick of sense.

Genny sat at the table, sewing the sleeve of a brown shirt, no doubt meant for him. He tried not to think about that and instead shook the ledger book in her general direction.

"What the hell is this?"

She looked at the book. "It was Henry's. Where did you find it?"

"I know it was Henry's. It was under the bed gathering dust for the last six months. Although I'm not sure anything you could have entered in here would make the numbers work." He paced around the table, trying to focus on how to fix the mess Blanchard had left.

"Numbers? I don't understand." Genny pointed at the book. "Is this for numbers?"

Lee stared at her. "It's an accounting ledger, meant for keeping track of money going in and out. Each time you spend money, you write it in, each time you add money, you write it in. Your husband apparently did it when he felt like it because nothing balances in here at all."

"I'm sorry, Lee, I don't know anything about it. It's important, right?" She looked so earnest he couldn't help but believe she didn't know what was supposed to be done. Most women were not privy to the financial workings of a business, but Genny was so smart, he'd thought she might have taken over after Henry died.

"Yes, it's very important. This is what tells you how much money you have so you can make sure you can buy things you need for the farm, for yourselves, as well as any food you need. Without knowing how much you have, there's no way to know when it will simply run out."

All color leached from her face, making the cinnamon freckles stand out. "Are you saying we have no money?"

"I don't know to be honest. It's such a mess, it will likely take me several days to figure out what he did." Lee set the book on the table. "I'll be happy to do what I can, and then maybe show you how to do it."

She bit her lip and looked at the book with a frown. "I don't know. Arithmetic isn't something I can do."

"A child can do simple arithmetic, Genny. You just have to take the time to sit down and do it."

"I've never learned how." She turned away and nearly put the shirt up to her nose as she stitched it.

Lee knew he'd been lucky in getting a good education, mostly due to Gideon's father paying for a tutor. He didn't know much about her childhood, but it apparently didn't involve learning basic math skills.

"I can teach you."

Her shoulders sagged a bit. "No, I don't think you can."

Lee picked up a chair and sat beside her. "If I can learn to do farm chores with one hand, you can learn to keep a ledger." He opened the book on the table and pointed to a page of entries. "See here? He writes down some things like flour, sugar and coffee from Marchison's, but then there's nothing here as to what this money was spent on."

Genny backed away from the table, shaking her head. "I don't know what he used money for, but it was probably booze and whores."

"Booze and whores?" Lee turned the ledger so he could look at it again. Maybe she was right. If he put together the missing entries, he might figure out exactly how much Henry Blanchard pumped into Aphrodite's. "Can you look at the dates and tell me if he, uh, wasn't here at the farm?"

She stood up and walked toward the kitchen. "No, I can't. I won't."

Lee picked up the book, frustrated with her refusals. Genny knew her husband frequented whores, that much was apparent, she didn't need to act as if she was unable to see her husband's infidelity in black and white. She was tougher than that. He brought the book toward her.

"Just look. It won't take but a few minutes." He held the book in front of her.

She slapped it down so hard, his hand stung. The book landed with a bang on the wood floor and echoed in the quiet cabin. "I said no."

"Why the hell not?" He picked up the book and wondered if she had really gotten over her husband's death. Maybe Genny had loved him too much to even contemplate his stepping out on her.

"Why not? My husband was a pig, a barely human man who spent his time whoring and drinking. I know where the money went. It doesn't take a smart person to know. I've got a farm that's falling apart, a crop to be brought in by one man, me and a little girl, I don't know how much money I have or if we'll survive the winter." She took a breath and Lee realized she was trembling. "Oh, and I can't read or write either, much less do simple arithmetic like a child."

With that she walked out the door, leaving Lee to stand there feeling like he'd kicked her. She couldn't read or write? He'd had no idea. Judging by the way she spoke, she had a vocabulary better than most farm wives. Didn't he feel like a complete ass. Again.

Lee set the ledger on the table and went in search of Genny. She was in the back garden pulling up weeds with a vengeance, and he was glad not to be a weed in her chokehold.

"I'm sorry." He didn't apologize often and here he was doing it twice in a matter of a few days. "I didn't mean to push you too hard, Genny. I just wanted to help. I'm not good with words or people and tend to annoy even when I'm not trying to. One thing I can do is arithmetic, and keeping books. The numbers, they just make sense to me."

She continued yanking up weeds, ignoring him and his apology. Lee wished Jake could whisper in his ear what to say. The redheaded devil had been the most suave of them, charming ladies right and left until Gabby had charmed him. Lee couldn't charm a rock.

"Please, Genny."

She stopped pulling up weeds and let out a sigh that made his heart twitch. "My mother never took me to school or taught me any of that kind of thing. She thought it only important I talked like a lady." Genny sat back on her heels. "Truth is I'm as ignorant as these weeds."

Lee squatted next to her, realizing there was much more bubbling inside Genny than anger over a cheating husband. She had a lot of secrets and they weighed her down. He cupped her cheek, the soft skin fitting perfectly in his palm.

"I'll teach you to read and write. Sophie too if you like. We had a tutor growing up so we had all of that crammed down our throats. It'd be nice if it did someone else some good too." He swallowed, trying to find the right words. "I want to help, Genny. Please let me."

Lee didn't realize how hard it would be to offer help to this proud woman. She nuzzled his hand, then landed a kiss on the base of his thumb. Skitters of desire replaced the discomfort of his clumsy attempt at an apology.

"All right, I'd be pleased if you'd teach me and Sophie. She hasn't been to school and I couldn't teach her." Genny offered him a tremulous smile. "Seems like you coming here to work on the farm was exactly what we needed."

Lee stood quickly and offered her his hand. He wasn't exactly what anyone needed, but he could try and help the widow Blanchard in any way he could.

The next week passed by quickly. Lee spent an hour or two each night teaching Sophie and Genny the alphabet and numbers. They practiced writing their names and sounding them out. Genny admitted to being a bit embarrassed to be learning her letters at her age, but Sophie was excited to have her as a fellow student.

Lee sat beside Genny at the table, watching as she sounded out the letters in the McGuffey's Reader. The "b" was especially difficult to watch because she moved her lips as if she were kissing. He wanted her to be kissing him instead of him teaching her to read.

Why had he ever agreed to it? She was capable of finding someone else to teach her and Sophie. Yet he continued each night, torturing himself and knowing what he wanted was to taste those lips again even as they sounded out the word ball.

It was the "l" that made his dick roar to life. Her mouth, oh God, and that tongue. Sheer torture, absolutely sheer torture. If only he hadn't tasted that mouth or known exactly how that tongue felt pressed against his own.

Genny looked at him expectantly and he realized she'd asked him a question. Yet he'd been lost in a fantasy of how deep she could take his dick into her mouth. Jesus Christ.

"I'm sorry, what did you say?"

She raised her brows as if to let him know she wasn't unaware of the nature of his woolgathering. "I said how am I doing?"

"Oh, you're doing great." He managed a smile even as he tried to tell his wayward stiffness to calm down. Being next to her was bad enough, but he had to go and watch her mouth for an hour.

"Hmm, well good." She gestured to Sophie, who was

currently writing her letters on an old slate Genny had found in Henry's trunk. "And how is she doing?"

The girl was so bright, it was almost impossible to keep up with her. As an adult, Genny was more difficult to teach because she was pretty much set in her ways. Stepping back into a learning mode was hard for anyone over the age of sixteen. But Sophie was a marvel. She already knew all her letters and numbers, even took time out each afternoon to practice them again and again.

"She's brilliant."

Genny closed the book and peered at him, a frown marring her face. "Are you saying that because you are distracted by me or do you really mean it?"

"I mean it. She's smarter than both of us put together. Pretty soon she's going to pass me and we'll have to put her in a real school."

He must've said something wrong because Genny's expression shuttered closed against him.

"She's not going to a real school. Ever." She picked up the book, but her eyes moved too rapidly across the page. Obviously she was only trying to avoid the conversation.

"Why not? What are you afraid of?" He pushed the book back to the table until she let go of it.

"I don't want her to suffer for being who she is."

"I don't understand what that means." Lee looked at Sophie. "She's perfectly normal and very smart. Do you think the children at school will tease her or something? That's normal, you know."

Genny shook her head. "No, that's not what I'm worried about. Sophie is, well, different than other kids. She's outspoken and stubborn, and she curses like a cowboy."

"I've noticed that." Lee wondered how the hell the brat had picked up such a colorful vocabulary.

"Henry didn't care who was around when he cussed. She grew up using cuss words the way ordinary folks say hello or good morning." Genny glanced at her daughter. "I tried to teach her right but Henry, well, he didn't like me spoiling her. Said it was good enough for a bastard like Sophie."

Lee realized what she'd said and it rang like a bell in his head. "What do you mean a bastard like Sophie?"

Genny's cheeks colored. "It was just the way he talked. He didn't mean nothing by it except that she was just a farm girl, didn't need pretty speech or fancy clothes."

It was the first time Lee knew for certain Genny had lied to him. She sucked at it. As much as he wanted to find out why she lied, he didn't want to push the topic. He could tell she was done talking about it when she stood up and ushered Sophie to get ready for bed.

A bastard? How could Sophie be a bastard if Genny and Henry had been married?

Lee was surprisingly good and patient as a teacher. Genny found her heart slipping farther and farther into his pocket with each passing day. He was a good man and he had so much to offer, if only he'd realize it.

The biggest problem Genny faced was that they were never alone, and that was Lee's doing.

He started each day before her, leaving the cabin so early the moon was still in the sky, even took his meals in the evenings after their lessons. It was ridiculous and it was beginning to annoy her. They were good for each other. So she took it upon herself to make him understand that instead of waiting for him to come to his senses.

She had made biscuits and put the milk jug in the stream behind the house to cool it. The day Genny had asked Gabby for help, her friend had confided to her Lee liked cold milk almost as much as she did. In fact, Gabby had been surprised Lee was drinking coffee instead of milk. At first, Genny thought it was odd a man liked milk, but the more she got to know him, the more endearing it was. A sharp contrast to his rough exterior. Genny wanted to surprise him with a glass of it and warm biscuits with honey.

Carrying a basket with a milk bottle, honey jar and biscuits, she crept into the barn and closed the door behind her. Sophie had been following Lee around all week and was exhausted enough to take a nap every day. For the most part, Genny was alone with Lee during those precious nap times.

Newly clean, the barn looked wonderful and actually smelled like a barn instead of an outhouse. Ned seemed happier, if that were possible, and Lee's horse was amenable to the stall he called home too.

Lee had been sorting through the tools Henry had accumulated. There were a bunch of hand tools, some equipment for the fields and a tangled pile of tack that may or may not actually be useful. Most of it was in the tack room or on the bench at the back wall of the barn. The shadowed interior was cool in the warm, late-summer afternoon.

She heard him mumbling to himself, or rather cursing under his breath, as she approached the back of the barn. She had to hide a smile when she heard him sigh almost as dramatically as Sophie did. Although he called her "brat" and seemed to barely tolerate her, Genny knew he'd taken a liking to Sophie. She was a wonderful girl even if she tested everyone's limits sometimes.

Genny came around the corner and saw Lee peering at the

cradle, the tool used to harvest the wheat. Henry had been too cheap to buy a mechanical reaper so he usually hired a couple of farmhands to harvest the wheat with the cradles he stocked in the barn.

"It's called a cradle."

He started at the sound of her voice and scowled mightily. "You need to wear a bell, woman. Stop sneaking up on me."

She smiled at his grumpy response. "I brought you an afternoon treat." Holding up the basket, she headed for the workbench. "Sophie's taking a nap and I just made these biscuits. They smelled so good I thought you might want one."

As she laid out a cloth on the bench, he watched her, his unreadable expression never wavering.

"I brought honey too and I hope you don't mind, but I was thirsty for milk."

His eyes widened at the sight of the bottle covered with condensation. "It looks cold," was all he said.

"Oh it is. I learned from Gabby to keep it in the stream and it stays cool even without a root cellar." Another thing Henry had been too lazy to dig out. All she had to store vegetables and roots in was a small trapdoor beneath the kitchen.

"Hmm, I guess I could use a drink, even if it is milk."

Genny hid the smile at his casual attempt at pretending he didn't want the milk. She poured some into the two mason jars she'd brought and handed one to him. As she slathered honey on a few biscuits, he drank the entire glass. When he realized what he'd done, his eyes widened and he looked at her guiltily.

"I brought plenty. Don't worry." She handed him a biscuit and took the jar to refill it.

Other than lesson times, they hadn't been alone all week. It was the first time in days he hadn't run the other direction when she entered the room if Sophie wasn't present. Milk was apparently a magic potion. He leaned against the bench and munched on the biscuits, alternately taking normal sips of milk.

"This thing is called a cradle?" He pointed at the reaper lying on the bench.

"Yes, it's a cradle. These long fingers attached to the handle, which I think is called a snath, let the wheat fall through so they lay down in a row for collection." She ran her fingers along the handle and his gaze followed their path. "The handle is long enough to be able to stand up as you cut the wheat."

"Ah, I see." He stuffed the rest of the biscuit in his mouth then licked his fingers. "Probably should've washed my hands first but damn that was good."

Genny smiled. "I'm glad you liked it." She slid closer to him. "I wanted to come out here and see you. I think you've been avoiding me, Lee."

"I spend time with you every night," he protested.

"Now you know that's not what I mean. Learning letters and numbers isn't spending time together." She held his chin until he looked at her. As her hand left his chin, the sound of his whiskers scraping her skin was loud in the quiet barn. "You've been hiding from me."

He frowned. "No, I've been busy working on getting this farm back in shape. I've got to start harvesting in a few days, right?"

She scoffed at his excuse. "That doesn't mean you have to get out of bed with the moon."

"I get up early because—"

"Or lock the bedroom door."

His gaze skittered around the room, landing anywhere but on Genny. The man apparently could not lie to her. "I don't want you to throw your life away on someone like me."

"Isn't that for me to decide?"

"I thought it best for both of us." He shifted away from her, but she followed. "People in town will think I took advantage of you."

Genny chuckled without humor. "Not likely. No one in town really knows me or likes me, Lee, except maybe Gabby and Mr. Marchison. After living here eight years, I'm more of a stranger than you are."

"I don't understand." He stopped moving away and looked at her with a puzzled expression. "Did your husband keep you prisoner here at the farm?"

"No, I chose to keep myself here." She had started the conversation to test him, and now she'd opened up the door to the past which lurked behind her every second of every day. "I'm not the pristine widow you think I am, Lee. I'm trash from the streets of New Orleans."

Her heart pounded as she let all the feelings she kept buried inside come creeping up her throat. So many nights she wondered if the first half of her life would ever fade from her memories. Obviously they never would. Deep wounds become permanent scars.

"Everybody has a past. Hell, I should've been dead ten times over already. Stupid, reckless ass that I am, I lost my arm six weeks before the war ended after years of fighting every damn day." He laughed without humor. "Nothing in your life compares to the idiocy of mine."

Genny knew he'd given her the opportunity to back away, to keep her secrets buried, but she didn't want to. If there were any chance they could be together, he had to understand exactly who she was and where she'd come from.

"My mother came from a nice family in Louisiana. She had the unfortunate luck to fall in love with a gambler from New Orleans who'd come to visit at her parents' plantation. She gave herself to him and he left her with a babe in her belly." Genny perched on a barrel, sitting on her hands so Lee wouldn't see them shaking. "She followed him to New Orleans only to discover he was already married. She didn't care, she just wanted to be with him, no matter how much shame or abuse he heaped on her. My father was a bastard through and through. He set her up in a house in the red-light district and sold her to his friends. She let him turn her into a common whore, or not so common because the society men who fucked her did it with gloves on their hands and left her with scars."

Lee watched her, not moving from his spot, the leftover milk in the jar beside him. "You knew this as a child?"

"How could I not? I grew up with my father coming by to ignore me and bed my mother. This was Sunday only. The rest of the week, men would come by with the 'secret password' he gave them to use my mother's services. Each of them had their own nasty way of getting their satisfaction, from whips to candle wax, and some of them were sodomites. Thank God I wasn't a boy." The laugh that came from within her was laced with pain and bitterness, but she let it loose, glad to have some of it gone. "Sometimes they even wanted me to watch."

"Jesus Christ," he breathed.

"By the time I was ten, there were men who wanted to bed me, even begged her for the experience. They liked them young and tight, don't you know. She had begun to like liquor a bit too much, and spent most of her time either in bed with the men, drinking with them around it, or passed out on it. I was raised by a housekeeper named Mrs. Markum who pitied me enough to make sure I was fed and took baths. I think my father might have paid her to do it." She shrugged at the memory of the cold, thin woman who served her meals and scrubbed her raw with a brush in the tub. "One night, one of the men came by but my mother was too drunk to service him so he raped her. I tried to stop him, but he slapped me, then raped me too."

Lee stepped toward her, but she held up a hand to stop him. "Let me finish. I want you to understand just what a wonderful person I am. I can't let you touch me until I finish, and then you might not want to touch me."

"Okay, I'll stay right here then." He moved over and sat on the barrel facing her.

Genny took a deep breath and swallowed back the tears of pity that threatened. Self-pity brought her nothing in her life except heartache, there was no need to let it loose again, especially now.

"It took me some time to recover and that was only because Mrs. Markum called a doctor. I found out who the man was, stole money from my mother and hired two street thugs to kill him."

She let that information sink in, not daring to look Lee in the eye. He had to know and she had to tell him everything.

"I never went without a knife to protect myself after that. When my mother found out what I'd done, she slapped me and told me never to tell my father. She didn't care that I'd been raped or that I'd had a man killed. She only cared that the man she loved would never find out how his friend was killed, as if he ever loved her enough to care. I existed in a world you can't even imagine, Lee. It all came to an end when she sold me to Henry for a hundred dollars."

"Pardon me?" His voice was incredulous.

"You heard me right. Henry was a widower who wanted a

tight vessel in his bed and on a trip to New Orleans, he visited his cousin. After spending some time with us, he offered to buy me and she accepted without a backward glance. I let Henry do what he needed when he needed to, cooked for him, and cleaned for him. Everything changed when I had Sophie." She paused as emotion washed over her. Her daughter was the person who had saved her. "There wasn't anyone in my life who knew me, wanted me, or loved me until Sophie. She loved me unconditionally, gave me every kiss and hug she could. Henry had trouble getting his business done in bed with me after a few years, so he went to town for company. I was never so glad to hear my husband was whoring."

Genny closed her eyes, remembering when she found out about Henry's death. "Doctor Barham came out to the farm to tell me Henry had died at Aphrodite's. He wasn't a good man, Lee, and I was glad he was gone. Two men had died in my life, one by my doing, the other by my wishing. I'm more of a black widow than a woman to love and cherish."

This time she couldn't stop the tears so she let them flow freely down her cheeks. Lee didn't need to think she was an upstanding citizen deserving of the town's respect. She was simply a piece of trash from a whore's womb who was lucky enough to have her husband die and leave her a beautiful daughter and a rundown farm.

Lee could have tried to pat her on the back and tell her it would be all right. Yet he didn't and she was glad for it. Instead, he handed her the cloth from the bench and held her hand until the silent sobs passed. He might pretend to be a bear and a mean-spirited bastard, but Genny knew better.

She meant what she'd told Zeke. Lee was a good man and she could love him so easily. She'd never loved a man before, but she'd never met a man as damaged as she was.

"That's quite a tale, Genny," he finally said, breaking the silence. "I've only got one thing to ask you. You gonna finish that biscuit?"

Genny's laugh burst from her throat, which was still tender from the tears. He hugged her then, tucking her beneath his chin and simply holding her. She knew there'd be no locked door that night.

Chapter Seven

The moon shone brightly through the lacy white curtains on the tiny window. Lee shifted uncomfortably on the bed, his body still awake, eager for what it shouldn't have—Genny. She'd told him a hell of a story about her life, but she'd been an innocent child, a pawn in the game of adults who should have done better by her. Lee wasn't any better than they were. He didn't deserve a woman who he could say "Fuck you" to.

It was as if he had a volcano inside him that just exploded at will, spewing hot lava all over everyone closest to him. When she'd cried in the barn, he didn't know what to do, so he just let her cry. God knew he wanted to break something and tear up New Orleans looking for the sorry-ass parents of hers. His anger knew no bounds.

Zeke had dealt with it for years somehow, but he didn't take much shit from Lee, never had even when he was just barely a teenager taking care of their family. Lee sighed and rubbed his palms against gritty eyes. It was the middle of the night and he hadn't slept a wink, and he was hungry. After their afternoon snack, Genny had left him alone in the barn. He'd wanted to say thank you for the cold milk and biscuits, which happened to be his favorite, but hadn't. Instead he spent time figuring out how to use the cradle, then walked around the farm for hours.

It helped him understand how the fields were laid out, what obstacles were around the property and just how much fucking work had to be done. Of course he'd told Sophie to tell Genny he wouldn't be there for supper. Coward that he was, he still didn't know what to say to her.

He hadn't eaten supper and his stomach yowled into the quiet night. Genny kept the leftover bread wrapped in a towel near the sink. Maybe if he just crept out real quick and got a piece he'd be able to sleep. As he reached for the doorknob, he thought about putting on his drawers, but decided against it. The house was silent as a tomb and it would take longer to get dressed than to snag a bit of bread.

The inky blackness of the night was only broken by patches of moonlight shining through the meager window. Lee stood in the doorway, allowing his eyes to adjust before he went any farther. No need to break his leg and add to the fun.

Finally, he could see the barely discernible outline of the furniture and started forward. He went slowly as to minimize the noise and any injuries. By the time he reached his destination, he'd only stubbed his toe twice, which he considered a fabulous victory. The bread would taste even better for it.

He stared into the darkness as he unwrapped the bread as fast as he could, trying not to think. If he didn't turn his mind off and stop the thoughts from crowding him, he'd never get any sleep.

"Lee."

He started at the sound of his name. Maybe he'd fallen asleep standing there and dreamed hearing her call his name. However when cool hands slid up his back, he dropped the bread and recognized it was no dream.

"Genny?"

What the hell was she doing? Did the woman have no sense? There was no reason she should be within ten feet of him, much less touching his buck-naked body in the kitchen.

"You're so warm."

Hell, he was going to be hotter than a prairie fire in about two minutes.

"This isn't a good idea," he forced himself to say.

"Mmm, I was never much for good ideas. In fact, my mama always used to say I was a bad idea walking." She kissed the center of his back and he closed his eyes, savoring the soft heat of her lips.

"Genny, you should go back to bed."

She chuckled, a warm puff against his skin. "That's the whole idea, cowboy. Only I planned on joining you. Much to my surprise, you weren't there."

No, I was too busy thinking about you to sleep. "I meant, you should go back to your bed."

"Ah, but that's where I was going. Remember, you're sleeping in my bed." She wrapped her arms around his waist and he realized two things at once—she was naked and her nipples were harder than diamonds.

"You can't, I mean, we can't. Genny," he sputtered, unable to even form a doggone sentence.

"Oh yes, we can. We have no reason not to be together, Mr. Blackwood." She reached down and took hold of his already rock-hard dick. "Besides, you're dressed for the occasion."

Lee barked out a laugh, then clapped his hand over his mouth lest he wake Sophie up. Who knew what the child would do if she found them like this?

Genny walked around him, trailing her hand along his waist until she faced him. He could barely see the pale gleam of her face in the blackness. She leaned forward and licked his nipple.

"Geeeeeeeeeennnny." Each time he tried to say her name, she nipped, scratched or bit a nipple. He jerked around like a puppet, his dick slapping against his stomach as he had no luck controlling his response to her ministrations.

"Mmmm, salty and sweet. I wonder what color they are?" She stroked him. "One of these days we're going to do this in bright sunlight so I can see what I'm tasting."

Before he knew what she was about, she dropped to her knees and took him in her mouth. Damn fool that he was, he almost came immediately, but he beat it back, biting his lip and clenching his fist until he could concentrate on exactly what she was doing. And it was like an angel had descended from heaven to be his for the night.

In the shadows, he couldn't see, he could only feel. Her hand cupped his balls, gently massaging them as her thumb pressed against the base of his staff. The warm heat from her tongue and her lips surrounded him, sucking him deep toward her throat. Her teeth lightly skittered along the length of him as she bobbed up and down, alternately nibbling and swirling her tongue.

He put his hand on her head, and the soft waves curled around his fingers as if recognizing him. Lee reveled in the feeling of having this smart, beautiful woman on her knees pleasuring him, just for the sake of doing it. She made little lapping noises like a kitten as she alternately played and then tortured him.

No woman had ever simply sucked him without payment, and even then he could tell the whores didn't enjoy it. It was money for fucking, and they did it to avoid starving. Genny did this because she wanted to, and he damn sure wanted her to.

"You're quite hard, Mr. Blackwood." She squeezed the base as she licked the top of his dick like it was a sucker.

Lee grunted, at a loss for how to respond. The woman had a magical mouth, and he was wondering how long he'd be able to stand upright, much less hold back his orgasm. But he did because he wanted to make love to her.

Make love.

Not hardly, but it was at least making like. He liked Genny, respected her and surely wanted her. She pulled him deep into her mouth, sucking so hard he knew she could already taste his seed.

"You need to stop now, Genny." It almost killed him to say that. "I won't make it to the bed if you don't."

She gentled her movements, lightening her touch until she was kissing the tip of his throbbing erection. "Sometime soon, I won't let you stop me."

Now that made the stupid thing jump again, this time slapping her in the cheek. She giggled and a laugh bubbled up his throat in response. So this was what being happy felt like. He didn't remember it as so amazing and pure. It was all Genny, leading him by the hand, or by the dick in this case, and showing him exactly what happiness was.

The woman was pure magic.

She stood and grabbed his head for a hard kiss. "Now let's get to that bed." Latching onto his cock like it was a leash, she led him through the gloomy cabin until they reached the bedroom. After pulling him into the room, she shut and locked the door. She tugged him toward the bed. He didn't need the tug, but it damn sure felt good.

"Now, I was thinking I'd like a ride tonight." She pushed at his chest lightly, and he understood what she wanted.

He lay down, wondering just how this woman knew exactly what he'd been dreaming about doing with her. It was uncanny, and a bit frightening. He'd think about it later because right about then, all he wanted was to feel.

She climbed onto the bed slowly, kissing her way up his erection to his stomach. After a quick bite on the nipples, she reached his lips and teased him with light kisses as she straddled him. He felt the heat from her pussy as she leaned down to kiss him. Their mouths fused, her tongue thrusting into his mouth as she lowered herself to rub against his length.

Genny was wet enough to make them rub against each other easily, the crisp pussy hairs tickling him with each slow slide. "You feel good, cowboy. So good."

"Not as good as you, Genny girl." He pushed against her, prompting her to gasp. Lee knew from Zeke that a woman had a kind of button on her cunt that was like a little dick, loved to be rubbed and licked. Next time he'd return the favor and try his hand, or his tongue rather, on her. "Put it in before it's over."

She bit his lip, making him remember just how wonderful her teeth were. "You're bossy."

"You're sexy. Now put it in." He reached down and rubbed her slick folds until she lifted up just enough for him to slide the head of his staff into her. God, he could hardly stand it, she felt so damn good. Then she sat up and took the length of him inside her.

Lee's breath caught in his throat and he'd have sworn his heart stopped for more than a moment. Heaven on Earth, that's what she was. So tight, hot and sweet. He groaned in sheer bliss.

"Did I do that? You really are big, oh so big." She breathed in short gasps as she began to move, sliding in slow, deliberate movements.

It was designed to torture him, of that he was certain. Lying on his back, he was at her mercy for the most part. He needed her to go faster, harder, so he started thrusting up each time she came down.

She let loose a moan he'd remember until the day he died, like a panther growl in the darkness. So he thrust against her again, then again until she caught his rhythm and abandoned the teasing altogether.

"Yes, oh yes, that's it." He grasped her hip on the right and pressed his arm into her thigh with his left. Then he realized if he pulled his knees up, he could really give her a ride.

"Oh God Lee, oh God, oh God." She grabbed her breasts, pinching the nipples, like a moonlight goddess come to life above him.

Lee felt his orgasm begin somewhere near his feet. It traveled up through his legs and surrounded his balls until he lost control. Genny shouted his name in a husky whisper as her cunt gripped his dick so tightly he came until his ears rang and his heart slammed against his ribs. Her legs squeezed him even as her own fingers squeezed her breasts. Lee watched her face as she came around him, the rapture, the bliss, the amazing woman who gave of herself freely.

As he returned back to Earth, he realized he may have lost something more than his inhibitions that night. He lost a piece of his heart as well.

Genny sat down gently, sore from her night's ride. She smiled into the depths of her coffee, hiding the happiness from Sophie's prying eyes. Lee had gotten up early again, made coffee and went to work. She should really be embarrassed for sleeping later than the sunrise, but the sex had been so overpowering, so amazing, it had plumb worn her out.

Sophie had to shake her awake, complaining her stomach was about to rub a hole in her backbone. Now the girl was happily stuffing her face with biscuits, ham and eggs while Genny's body still hummed with the truly satisfied feeling of a woman who'd been pleasured the night before.

"Why are you grinning at your cup, Mama?"

Genny couldn't stop the laugh from escaping. "It's a beautiful day and I'm happy, I guess."

"You're an odd duck today." Sophie said that so matter-of-factly, Genny's mouth dropped open. The child had never said such a thing before and Genny wondered if she'd ever cease to amaze her.

"Now where did you hear that?" Genny shook her head in wonder.

"Mr. Marchison. He said it about that lady who wears the hats and smells like mothballs." Sophie screwed up her face in imitation of Hettie. "You know the lady who yells at you if you touch her flowers."

"Now that's not polite. Miss Hettie is just proud of her roses." Genny agreed with Sophie's assessment, but she had to at least pretend to teach the child manners.

Sophie shrugged. "They have thorns that hurt you, like Mr. Blackwood. He's kinda pretty but he's got thorns too."

Before Genny could contemplate how the child could make such a comparison, an accurate one too, she continued on. "You love him, don't you?" Sophie stared at her, brow furrowed.

This time it was Genny's turn to stop and stare. "Pardon?"

The moppet nodded sagely then gobbled the bite of eggs. "You can marry him. It's okay, you know. I didn't like him to start, but he works hard even if he only has one arm. I think he'd be a better Daddy than Pa was."

Genny was astonished, truly astonished at her daughter's insight. The girl was amazing, and Genny was thankful for such a gift. "You've got it all figured out, haven't you?"

"We would live here like a real family again." Sophie stood up and kissed Genny on the cheek. "I want to be a family again. Mr. Blackwood makes you smile even if he does give you a rash on your neck."

Genny hid her embarrassment with a laugh, and Sophie headed toward the door, skipping and humming. A knock stopped her in her tracks. She looked back at Genny. "Sounds like trouble, Mama."

Genny shook her head. "That's silly. It's just someone coming to visit." Of course, they didn't receive many visitors at the farm so it was an unusual occurrence, but with Lee there, they had protection. She stood and walked over to the door, with less trepidation than she had in a long time.

When she opened it Sophie darted out and ran toward the barn. A man stood on the porch with dark hair and a fancy suit holding a silver-tipped cane. Her stomach dropped toward her feet when she recognized Mr. Newman from the bank in town. Did Henry have debt she didn't know about?

He smiled and Genny remembered just how handsome the man was. "Good morning, Mrs. Blanchard." With a wide smile and a nicely trimmed beard, he was probably thirty-five, unmarried and sought after by women in town. She'd never had a thought for catching his eye although she could see the appeal.

"Good morning, Mr. Newman. Please come in." She opened the door wider, feeling as if a passel of frogs were hopping around in her stomach. Henry had kept secrets, she was more than sure of that.

"Thank you. I apologize for dropping by so early. I have the copy of the information on the account at the bank Henry had maintained and thought I'd bring it by." He stepped in and went toward the table.

Genny couldn't imagine why he'd come all the way out to the farm with it, not that she could read it. It was odd enough to make her off balance. "Would you like some coffee?" Genny grabbed another cup from the shelf above the sink and poured some before he even got to the chair.

"Yes, that would be wonderful. Thank you." He sat down, settling the cane beside him.

Her breakfast forgotten and good mood completely gone, Genny slid into her chair with uneasiness riding her back. She looked at him expectantly.

"Oh yes, the paper." He pulled a folded paper from his inner coat pocket and handed it to her. "This is a copy of account information on the farm. Henry had a total of forty-seven dollars and thirteen cents left in the bank, which is now yours as his widow." He smiled, looking for all the world as if he was nervous.

While she was trying to figure out just how long forty-seven dollars would feed her and Sophie, she wondered what he had to be nervous about.

The front door burst open and Lee stood there, harness firmly attached to his arm and wearing the brown shirt she'd sewn for him. He looked so good, Genny's whole body clenched in remembrance of touching him, kissing him, tasting him. The man grew more sexy each time she saw him. The fact he'd made coffee this morning and let her sleep in let her know she'd been right about him. He wasn't the ogre he pretended to be. Genny had the fanciful notion he had come into the house to rescue her and her heart thumped hard at the thought.

Sophie stood behind him, peeking out from behind his legs.

Mr. Newman looked surprised to see Lee, whereas Lee looked very unhappy to see Mr. Newman. "Richard? What are you doing here?"

"I could ask you the same thing, Lee." Richard frowned. "What are you wearing?"

Lee glanced down. "It's, uh, a sleeve for cripples."

Genny was embarrassed by his crude response, but Richard only nodded. "It's a good design. Is it working?"

"Actually yes, and she is the lady with the magic needle." Lee pointed at Genny. "The brat had the idea."

"I ain't a brat," Sophie piped up from behind him.

Richard smiled, revealing a row of even white teeth. Genny couldn't help but appreciate his handsome visage. She still had no idea why the banker was there. He could have held the papers for her in the safe at the bank—there was no need to personally deliver them.

"What brings you here, Newman?" Lee closed the door and walked toward the table, his lean-hipped swagger reminding her of a mountain lion tracking his prey.

"I had some papers for Mrs. Blanchard." He gestured to the paper in Genny's hand. Why didn't he sound as if he was being completely honest? "And I thought I'd pay a social call while I was here."

Genny froze in place, as did Lee. Social call?

"Did you come here to court Mrs. Blanchard?" Lee scowled. "Is that what you're saying?"

Richard glanced at Genny, meeting her gaze with an earnest one of his own. "If she's amenable to it, yes I did."

She'd spent her life trying to figure out why God had put her on the Earth. Now she had become a landowner with a wheat farm, and a mother with a healthy child. Genny was amazed to see two men facing each other over her like fighting cocks. She marveled how life had decided to be strange and difficult.

"Me? You want to court me?" Genny knew she sounded as incredulous as she felt.

Richard offered her a shy smile. "You're a handsome woman, Mrs. Blanchard. It's been six months since your husband passed. I thought it an acceptable time to do so." He shook his head. "Unless you're not willing to have me court you."

"I'll leave you two lovebirds alone then." Lee stomped out before Genny could answer, Sophie hot on his heels after a final scowl at Richard.

"I lost my wife ten years ago and realize life has gotten a bit too lonely in my house. I'll admit I've got a bum leg and a grumpy disposition in the morning."

Genny choked on the laugh that wanted to burst forth at the thought Richard considered himself grumpy. He had no idea what grumpy was.

"Otherwise, I own the bank and have all my teeth." He let loose a small chuckle. "Sounds like I'm offering myself up at a horse auction."

This man had no idea who she was, where she'd come from or even how damaged she was, even if it was all on the inside. "Mr. Newman, I don't know what to say. I'm flattered, truly I am. You're a handsome man and I've seen more than one lady in Tanger cast her eye in your direction. Why me?" She couldn't help but be blunt, something she and Lee had in common.

"That's a fair question. I noticed you after I first arrived in Tanger, when your husband brought you into the bank. He was taking care of his business and you stayed by the door with your daughter, playing jacks on the floor." He smiled, his blue eyes crinkling at the corners. "You didn't seem to care much about money or about anything else but being a good mother. That told me a lot about your character. Then, well, I had a few conversations with Gabby Sheridan."

Was he blushing? Genny had never had such a strange conversation with a man before. He'd noticed her over a year ago, yet he'd waited until she was a widow for six months before he came courting.

"Mr. Newman—" she began.

"Richard please, call me Richard." He put his hand on hers.

The warmth from his skin felt comfortable, but there wasn't even a smidge of spark. When she touched Lee, it felt as if she'd stuck her hand in hot coals. That alone told her what her answer should be to Richard's request to court her. Yet what promises had she made to Lee? None except with her body and deep in the recesses of her heart.

Genny looked at Richard, the man with money, stability and an apparent attraction to her. Any woman with a lick of common sense would smile pretty and snatch him up with both hands. She, unfortunately, was never known for having common sense, and who could blame her? No one in her life had taught her what common sense was.

Richard was looking at her, waiting for her to speak. What was she going to tell him?

Lee slammed the post digger into the ground with as much force as he could muster. It wasn't as much as he could have three years ago, but more than he could have two weeks ago without the harness. The nail was firmly hanging onto the wooden handle as he repeated the process. The corral needed a lot of work, and replacing the missing posts was only the first step.

Sophie sat on the ground near the gate, watching him work, fetching things from the barn as he needed them. He tried not to think about Genny inside with Richard, what they were talking about, or what they were doing.

Sweat rolled down the side of his face and down his back as the sun rose in the sky. Thumping the shit out of the dirt should make him feel better, but it didn't. What he really wanted to do was run back in the house and throw Richard out on his ass. The banker didn't deserve it, of course. He was actually a good friend to the Blackwoods and a good choice for a widow like Genny.

That didn't stop Lee from wanting to beat on his chest and howl.

He set the post digger aside and wiped his brow on his sleeve. The replacement fence post sat on the ground a few feet away. It had been in the back of the barn, a bit musty but useable. Once upon a time old Henry must've thought he'd fix the corral. Good thing too, because he suspected Genny didn't have money to buy any lumber and certainly not the strength to make what she needed from the woods beyond the edge of the property.

Richard had enough to buy her an entire new corral and pay someone to build it. Lee dug the nail hook on his harness into the wood and pulled up, allowing him to pick up the post and carry it back to the hole.

"Don't offer to help or nothing, brat."

She stuck out her tongue at him. "I can't lift that thing."

Lee slid the post into place, guiding it with his legs as splinters dug into his knees. When it was set in the hole, he looked over at Sophie. "Now get your little fanny over here and fill in the dirt."

With a sigh, she scampered over and squatted beside him.

She was obviously used to sitting in and likely playing in the dirt.

"Mama likes you."

Lee snorted. "Is that why she's in the house courting with the rich banker?"

"She didn't invite him. Besides I told her to marry you."

"You did what?" He could hardly believe his ears.

"Told her to marry you." She let the dirt slide through her hands. "You make her smile."

The child's explanation was so simple yet it said so much.

"What did she say?" His heart thumped loudly and it wasn't from hard work.

"I dunno. That man got here and I left." Sophie looked up at him, her expression so much like Genny's, he realized then he was hopelessly lost, completely, utterly in love with Genny and her daughter. "I think you're a much better Daddy than Pa ever was."

Lee stared at the girl, more shocked than he could imagine. "Daddy?"

"Well, yeah, you teached me stuff like the alphabet and 'rithmatic, and made me do chores." Sophie sounded so matter-of-fact Lee choked on his spit.

"Your pa never did that?" Lee wouldn't be surprised, considering how much Henry hadn't done around the farm.

"No, he was hardly around. Sometimes he hit me and Mama. I didn't like him much even if he was my pa."

Lee tightened his hand on the fence post until his knuckles popped. Men who used their fists on women and children were lower than the bugs under rocks. Then he marveled at how amazing Genny was to be strong enough to survive a husband who beat her, ran around with whores and left her to starve on a farm. He wished Henry was still alive so he could beat the shit out of him.

God, to have a family, to have a woman to love, a brat under his feet. It was so much to wish for, to hope for. More than a one-armed fool deserved.

Lee focused on Sophie's hands instead of Genny, and what she might be doing in the house with Richard. It wasn't his business what they were doing, dammit. Just because he'd spent time in bed with Genny didn't mean shit. Genny needed a husband, one who could support her, not one who wore a handmade harness to do work around the farm. It didn't matter one whit that she'd been a child of two parents who hadn't been married or that she'd grown up in such a hellhole. She was a good woman who deserved better than what life had already given her. That didn't mean Lee or what he couldn't give her.

Lee was a temporary farmhand, fixing things up and bringing in the crop, that's all. He couldn't expect her to settle for him when she could have the most eligible bachelor in town next to Gideon. Richard was a good man and he'd treat Genny right.

"Need any help?"

He'd been focusing so hard on Sophie, he let out a shout when Genny spoke from behind him. Sophie giggled, the little sucker.

"No, I don't. Go back and entertain Richard." He looked down at Sophie who looked back up at him.

"Thorns are sharp today, Mama."

He had no idea what the brat was talking about, but she'd filled in the hole pretty well. "Now scoot back so I can stamp the dirt down."

Sophie got to her feet and waited by his side. He could feel Genny behind him, her stare glued to his back as he pulled the nail free with his right hand. He stamped the dirt as hard as he could, trying desperately to get rid of the anger bubbling inside him. It was as if he had absolutely no control over his temper. If she stayed, he might just let loose on her again.

"Fetch me that mallet with the fat top from the barn." Lee probably should have been surprised Sophie was doing what he told her to, but he was too distracted by Genny.

After the girl went into the barn, Genny touched his shoulder. He flinched.

She sucked in a breath. "We made no promises, Lee."

"Don't you think I know that? Jesus, you can choose whatever you want to do with your life, and Richard is obviously a good choice." Lee's voice felt as rusty as the nails he'd pulled out of the old fence post. "We enjoyed each other's company is all. I don't expect more than that. Richard is the best man for you and we both know it."

He trembled as he waited for her to walk away, to tell him to go to hell, anything. His stomach clenched so hard he tasted bile in his throat, even as his heart hoped for more, so much more.

Genny watched him as he spat words at her, trying to drive her away and into Richard's arms. The logical choice would have been to do just that, but he was halfway back to Tanger by now. She'd already let her heart make a choice.

She laid her hands on his shoulders, not caring that he was covered with sweat or shaking. He made a noise when her forehead pressed against the center of his back, something between a moan and a sob. Genny hadn't been given much in life, she'd taken what she could before, but this time, it had to be given. Lee had shown her what it meant to put everything he had into what he did, against all odds and common sense.

"Lee," she managed to get past the giant lump in her throat. "I don't want Richard."

He stilled and she was certain he was holding his breath.

"I want you. Hell, I think I even lo—"

Before she could finish her sentence, he swung around and yanked her against him. His lips came down hard on hers, branding her, telling her what he felt without words. She wrapped her arms around his neck and hung on to the sweaty, stinky man she'd gone and fallen in love with.

"Well at least the fancy man is gone. Mama, are you gonna marry the one-armed grumpy man?" Sophie's voice broke through the haze of emotion surrounding them.

They broke off the kiss and Genny looked into Lee's brown eyes. When she saw hope and love hidden behind the ridiculously long lashes, she knew the answer to the question.

"Why of course I am. That is if he'll have me."

She hadn't seen him smile, really smile, since he'd been at the farm. He was simply stunning, his beauty snatching the breath right from her body. Two weeks seemed like a lifetime, but it's all the time that had passed. Her life had changed so drastically since she'd driven Ned into Tanger to beg Gabby for help. She'd had no idea that simple trip would bring Lee into her life, into her heart.

Lee closed his eyes and leaned his forehead against hers. "Are you sure?" he whispered against her cheek.

"I've never been more sure of anything."

Lee kissed the end of her nose. "Then I guess I'll marry you."

Sophie clapped her hands together and hooted. Genny laughed as he picked her up and swung her around. She'd never felt so happy, so loved, so blessed.

Chapter Eight

The mood in the wagon on the way to Tanger was much different than the last trip to town weeks earlier. Sophie wasn't whining or complaining. In fact, she was singing songs under her breath as she perched on the seat between the two of them. Lee drove the wagon, holding the traces with his right hand while they were wrapped around the hook on his left.

Genny sat beside her daughter, happiness bubbling inside her like a spring. She held onto the feeling, savored how wonderful it felt. After many years of simply existing, Genny was finally living.

"Are we gonna go to the preacher today?" Sophie piped up.

Lee glanced over at Genny with a tiny smile. "Yeah, we'll see him today, but we'll have to wait until your mama gets a proper wedding dress before we get married."

"Oh, Mama doesn't care what she wears. That blue dress is good enough."

Genny laughed. "Well it might be nice to have a new dress. I can get material from Mr. Marchison and make something in a few days."

"I don't want to wait that long. Can't I be a Blackwood today?" Sophie crossed her arms and scowled at both of them.

Lee nudged her with his elbow. "Unofficially you are. In

fact, you can tell people you're Sophie Blackwood."

"Yay!" she whooped, while Lee and Genny smiled at her.

Life was nearly perfect, even if the farm was in bad shape, they needed money and help, and there wasn't enough food to last the winter. Genny didn't care one whit about those things, at least for the next day or two. She was getting married and this time, she did the choosing and the asking.

It was nearly dinnertime and there were plenty of folks out on the streets in Tanger. Many of them nodded, waved or called out a greeting to Lee and Genny. For the first time, Genny felt welcome in town and she attributed it to the man she'd asked to marry her.

"Why don't we stop at the restaurant and have dinner first?" Genny's stomach was finally settled enough to have food. It had been twisted up for days and now she felt as free as a butterfly in search of a flower.

"The restaurant?" His voice sounded strained.

"Doesn't your family own it? I thought Gabby told me you used to live there." Genny couldn't quite see his face with the black hat shading it.

"Yeah, I did." He blew out a breath. "I should have told you why I left."

Genny didn't know if she should be nervous or not. Zeke had told her quite a bit about Lee, but obviously not everything. "Sophie, climb in the back so Lee and I can talk."

"Do I have to?" she whined.

"Yes, now scoot." Lee was already acting like her father. It warmed Genny's heart to see how well the two of them had taken to each other. She'd had doubts they'd get along at all when Lee first arrived at the farm—now he had become the father Sophie so desperately needed. It would devastate both she and Sophie if Lee left their lives.

After the girl grudgingly climbed into the back, Genny moved next to Lee so their thighs were touching. "Now tell me."

He slid a glance at her and she saw guilt in the depths of his brown eyes. "I rebuilt that restaurant with Zeke and my cousin Gideon. We own half of it together. The other half is owned by Cindy Cooley—she lives upstairs at the mill. Anyway, it burned down if you remember, and we rebuilt it, opened it and almost closed it within a month. None of us could cook worth a damn. We were lucky to convince Margaret Summers to be our cook."

He swallowed and licked his lips. Obviously whatever he had to say was about Margaret. Her stomach tightened at the thought.

"I, uh, sort of asked her to marry me in the spring. She said no and I left the restaurant for Gideon to run alone." He said it fast as if it was painful and he wanted it done quickly.

Genny wasn't sure if she should be jealous, upset or angry. He'd asked this woman to be his wife. "Do you love her?"

Lee blew out a breath. "Margaret was the first woman to treat me like a man, not a cripple. I think I wanted it to be love." He turned to look at her for the first time since he'd starting talking about Margaret. "It wasn't."

He was telling her he loved her without actually saying the words. She touched his cheek. "I love you too, Lee." His eyes widened so she leaned forward and kissed him quick. "Now let's go to the restaurant and have dinner. I want to meet the rest of your family."

"Aw, stop kissing already. Ain't you supposed to be married before you do all that?" Sophie stuck her head between them.

Genny kissed her daughter's forehead and tugged one braid. "Mind your business, Sophie."

"Are you sure?" Lee was asking more than one question and Genny knew it.

"Never been more sure of anything in my life."

With a heart lighter than he'd felt in his life, Lee pulled the wagon up behind the restaurant. She loved him. Holy Christ, she loved him. Nothing else mattered. Nothing.

While he released Ned from the traces, Genny helped Sophie down and straightened them both out. The girl popped up beside him and took hold of the horse's bit.

"I can bring him to the stable. It's important to take care of your horse so he can take care of you." She blinked up innocently as Lee stared down at her.

Lee wondered if the girl would ever stop surprising him. She recited word for word what he'd told her the first day they'd been together. Perhaps things were finally working out and God would gift him with what He'd withheld for so long.

After getting Ned settled they went into the restaurant. Margaret was nowhere to be seen, but at least half the tables were full. A young girl with dark brown hair Lee didn't recognize was serving plates of hot food. He nodded to a few folks as he made his way to the kitchen, Genny and Sophie behind him.

He pushed open the door to find Margaret slicing meatloaf at the table. Her apron was smeared with flour and gravy, and her hair had the same frizzy halo it always did. Lee had wondered what he'd feel when he saw her again, if he would be angry or hurt, but he didn't feel either of those things. He felt relief.

She glanced up and stopped slicing. "Lee. I didn't expect you." Her gaze moved behind him. "Hello."

Genny walked around him and held out her hand. "Hello.

I'm Genevieve Blanchard. I'm happy to meet you."

Margaret set down the knife and shook Genny's proffered hand. "Hello, I'm Margaret. Welcome to Elmer's Restaurant."

Sophie looked up at him. "You'd better not change your mind and want to marry her. She's too pretty for you."

Lee was surprised when he barked out a laugh. "Meet Sophie. She's, ah, a girl who likes to speak her mind."

Genny swooped her up in a hug. "You have got to stop doing that, girl." Sophie squealed in her mother's arms.

Margaret smiled at Lee. "What's going on?"

Gideon's voice came from behind them. "I'd like to know the same thing."

Lee turned to his cousin. "Let's sit down for dinner. I've got a lot to tell you."

After introductions were done, they sat in the corner away from most diners and dug into the meatloaf and potatoes. Sophie didn't say much, but she ate every bite on her plate. Lee didn't remember eating beef when he was at the farm. Most times Genny served salted meat like ham and bacon, likely traded for flour or perhaps vegetables from the garden.

He made a vow to himself that this little girl who wanted him to be her pa would never go hungry. She was too precious to not know what meatloaf tasted like.

Gideon sipped coffee as he watched them eat. Lee knew his cousin was brimming with questions, but he was polite enough to keep them to himself until they finished dinner. Even if he should feel nervous, he didn't. Even if Genny wasn't perfect, she was perfect for him.

Gideon leaned over to Sophie. "I'll bet if you go in the kitchen, Miss Margaret might have apple pie."

The girl's head snapped up from just about licking the

gravy from her plate. She looked at her mother. "Mama, can I?"

"Yes, but stay in the kitchen and don't bother Miss Margaret. She's got lots of folks to feed." Genny smiled at Gideon as Sophie scampered off her chair and headed to the kitchen, braids flying behind her.

"She's a sweet girl." Gideon glanced between them. "Can I speak freely?"

Lee looked at Genny and she nodded. "Yes."

"Tell me what's going on. Zeke came by and said you were out working at a farm for the harvest. You haven't stepped foot in the restaurant for six months and now you appear with a family in tow and a smile on your face." Gideon leaned forward. "Lee, I haven't seen you smile in years."

Lee couldn't help but smile again. "I went out there to help Genny. Somehow in all the piles of horse shit and repairs, we sort of found each other."

Gideon's brows went up. "Found each other?"

Genny chimed in. "Mr. Blackwood, I don't know if you knew Henry Blanchard. He was not a good husband or father. When your cousin came to the farm, he showed me what it means to be cared for. I asked him to marry me."

"What?" Gideon blinked, his blue eyes wider than the plate on the table.

"She did." Lee shook his head. "I said yes."

This time it was Gideon's turn to smile. "You're getting married?"

"You're the first to know, but I need to tell Zeke next. Then we've got to see Gregory at the church."

Gideon whooped and picked Lee up into a bear hug, and this time, Lee didn't shy away. He embraced his cousin and absorbed the love he could finally accept.

The rest of the day was a blur of congratulations and smiles. They never made it to the church to talk to the preacher. Gregory would be there the next day so they decided to gather at the mill for supper. Gabby insisted on cooking for everyone and Genny helped her along with Naomi. Lee stood outside with Jake, Zeke and Gideon as the night creatures serenaded them.

"Married?" Zeke whistled. "I have to say I thought it might happen given the way you were falling for her, but I didn't expect you to show up a short time later and tell me you were getting married."

"She proposed to him, did he tell you that?" Gideon teased.

"She did?" Zeke hooted and slapped Lee on the back of the head. "What's wrong with you? Why didn't you ask her?"

Lee pushed his brother away, tolerant for the teasing but not willing to get beat on for it. "She asked me first. Besides, I'm getting the better part of this deal. That woman is stronger and braver than me. She's put me to shame with the steel in that spine of hers."

The men sobered instantly.

"Things were that bad with Henry?" Jake frowned. "I met him a few times and never liked him. Genny was always silent and Sophie was a shadow behind her."

"Not just Henry, but a lot of her life." Lee wasn't going to reveal what Genny had told him. It wasn't his right and he didn't want to betray her confidence. "I never met someone who took on so much shit head-on and didn't flinch."

"Then she's perfect for you because all you do is shovel shit." Zeke grinned and stepped out of reach when Lee tried to punch him.

"Well, she's at least chosen the right Devil. She's too much woman for Gid." This time Lee did the teasing.

All of them howled with laughter except Gideon. He pointed at Lee. "You'd better watch it, Cornelius. I'll bet you haven't even told her about your real name."

Lee's blood froze. "You wouldn't."

"Oh yes I would!" Gideon ran for the door with Lee hot on his heels. Zeke and Jake tried to trip him, but ended up falling in the door behind him.

Genny heard a commotion by the front of the house, but didn't pay much attention. The men were outside drinking whiskey and talking. Naomi made her feel as if she were already her sister-in-law. The blonde woman was so beautiful, it made Genny's eyes hurt to look at her for too long.

While Genny mashed the potatoes, Naomi set the table and Gabby sliced the roast. Beef twice in one day was almost sinful, but Genny wasn't about to refuse.

With a gigantic crash, the four men tumbled into the kitchen like a pack of puppies, punching, laughing and hollering at each other. She couldn't figure out what was so funny about acting foolish, but Gabby smiled while Naomi shook her head.

"What are you doing? Get up off my floor." Gabby waggled her finger at them. "You're tracking in mud, and God knows I don't want to clean it up."

"It's his fault, Gabby." Jake pointed at Lee. "He went after Gid and dragged me and Zeke into it."

"Why you redheaded liar! I did no such thing. Gid was going to tell Genny and I—" He stopped and stared at her, mouth open.

Genny raised her brows, waiting for him to explain exactly what they were doing and why he wanted to stop Gideon. "I'm all ears, Misters Blackwood."

"That leaves me out." Jake climbed to his feet, shaking off Lee's hold on his ankle.

Lee frowned up at Jake, then turned to push Zeke's legs off his. "Get off me." He looked guilty when he glanced at Genny. "It's nothing, really."

Zeke got to his feet and helped Gideon up off the floor. Both of them watched Lee with identical smirks.

"Is that right?" Gideon brushed off the front of his trousers. "Then you tell her."

Genny didn't know what to expect, but apparently the rest of them did. It couldn't be that bad, could it?

"Yeah, go ahead and tell her." Zeke smiled at Naomi. "You'd be surprised at how sexy your name can sound when it's whispered in the dark."

Naomi blushed and winked at her husband. Now Genny was really intrigued. What was Lee hiding?

He took her elbow and led her out to the mill where the machines were blessedly still for the night. She was starting to get nervous when he paced back and forth in front of the huge wheel while he ran his hand down his face.

"Just tell me, dammit."

He let out a huge sigh. "My real name isn't Lee."

"Is that all? That's the big secret that had you tussling on the ground like a five-year-old?" Relief washed over her. "Is it something horrible?"

"It's a big deal to me and Zeke. You see, our father wanted us to be pious men so he gave us Biblical names. We hated them and thought of short versions to use." Lee shrugged. "It became a game of sorts, make each other loco by using the real ones. I guess I kind of got lost in the memory of it."

She approached him and stopped the mad pacing with one touch on his chest. "There is absolutely nothing you can be named that would make me walk out that door. Although if your name was Delores, I might have to think about it." Genny chuckled as she pulled him close, pressing her belly into his, feeling the twitch of his cock beneath the trousers she'd made for him. "So are you going to tell me?"

Moments passed and she thought perhaps she needed to step back, concerned his first name would affect their marriage, silly as it sounded.

"Cornelius."

Genny had no idea about Biblical names since she'd never heard or read the Bible, but it didn't sound too bad to her. "I like it. Maybe your brother is right. We should test it out in the dark." She leaned forward, pushing her breasts into his chest, then leaned up to whisper, "Cornelius."

He shivered against her. Apparently Zeke wasn't mistaken at all.

"Say it again." His voice was husky with need.

She reached up to kiss him. "Cornelius." Genny lapped at his lips and he crushed her to him, hard and fast. Her body heated immediately, growing damp between her legs, her nipples hardening almost painfully. "We can't do this here," she breathed against his lips.

"I can't wait, Genny. I need you." It was the first time he'd ever admitted to her that he needed anything, much less to join with her.

She couldn't refuse.

He led her deeper into the mill so they were hidden from view by the giant wheel. Hopefully his family would leave them alone, thinking they were discussing Cornelius. She almost laughed at the silliness of it, but then he pressed his very hard cock against her and she wasn't feeling humorous any longer.

"Pull up your dress, God, hurry, Genny, hurry."

She heard him yanking at his trouser buttons, ones she'd made big enough to handle with one hand. She pulled up her dress and yanked down her drawers. She'd sewn up the slits in all her drawers years earlier to make Henry's access that much more difficult.

Genny made a note to open the slits back up for her new husband.

As she bent forward to take off the cotton drawers, her cheek brushed against his cock. He was hot, so hot, and harder than steel. She laved his staff, but he hauled her up before she could do more.

"Much as I love your mouth on me, darlin', I need to be inside you. Now." He pushed her up against the wall, and she wrapped her legs around him. His right arm made a shelf for her ass, even as he moved in. "Put it in, Genny."

She reached between them and guided the throbbing erection to her willing pussy. He entered her with one hard thrust. Genny's breath caught in her throat as her body closed around him in utter satisfaction.

Yes, yes, yes. This was perfect, this was meant to be.

Genny braced herself on the beams around her as his mouth captured hers in a fiery kiss. His tongue twined with hers as he began to move. The angle allowed him to enter her completely, to fill her until she couldn't tell where he ended and she began.

"You feel so good." He pumped into her, keeping her pinned to the wall behind her. She pushed down with each thrust up, taking him all.

Genny bit his lip as her body began to contract with

release. She'd never had an orgasm with a man inside her, until Lee. She'd never had an orgasm within minutes of having him inside her, until now. It was as if her body knew he was her soul mate, her perfect match, and took the joy along with the emotions to form a perfect song of pleasure.

"Now, Genny. Now," he whispered roughly. His whiskers scraped against her neck as he fucked her fiercely, so hard her head banged against the wall. He came with a husky groan and within seconds her body responded in kind.

Waves of ecstasy shook her, stretching out the pure bliss as it washed over her skin like a hard summer rain. She bucked against him, her nails digging into the wood beams. The only sound she heard was the frantic beating of her heart and the short staccato breaths she managed to suck in.

"Holy shit."

She chuckled softly. "Holy shit indeed, Cornelius."

He pressed his forehead into her breasts. "Now that was, ah, a perfect way to spend five minutes."

Lee let her down slowly until her legs could support her, wobbly as they were. Genny and Lee took a few minutes to try to straighten their clothes, then he suggested walking out to the river to perform a discreet wash. Genny followed him outside, where the sound of the river was soothing. He showed her a small pool beside the mill where water had been warmed by the afternoon sun.

The water was perfect temperature by then, not too warm but cool enough on her heated flesh. The very fact they'd been inside fucking against the wall in the mill made a short laugh escape.

"Something funny?" He was barely discernible in the gloom around them.

"No, just a happy thought." She took his arm as they

150

walked back to the mill. "Life is just so perfect, Lee. I just want to keep it tucked close to my chest and hang on."

He tightened his grip on her arm. "Yeah, me too."

Supper was a lively affair with everyone teasing, laughing and enjoying the feast. Toasts were made in Genny and Lee's honor. She couldn't remember ever being so relaxed and happy. Lee's family was wonderful and she already felt connected to them.

When a knock sounded at the door during dessert, none of them expected Margaret to be standing in the doorway. She looked at Gideon and Lee with enough worry to make Genny's stomach flip.

Gabby took Margaret's hand. "Please, come in. Do you want some coffee or peach pie? It's not nearly as good as yours but—"

"No, I need to talk to Lee and Gideon." She nodded toward the door. "Outside please."

Genny stood as the men did. "I'm coming too."

Margaret looked at Lee and he nodded. "Okay. Let's all go outside."

Genny's heart thumped, wondering what it was that made Margaret leave the restaurant during the supper crowd to find Lee and Gideon. The fireflies lit up the night as Margaret paced on the porch.

"I'm sorry to interrupt your meal."

"Get on it with it, Margaret. We know each other better than to apologize." Gideon put his hands on his hips. "What's going on?"

"There's a woman and a man in the restaurant. She says her name is Camille." Margaret shot a glance at Genny. "And the man with her is named Willard. She's looking for Henry

Blanchard."

The world seemed to open up and swallow Genny whole as she tried to hold on to something. She looked at Lee and everything started turning black, then the ground rushed up at her.

Lee carried her upstairs to his old room, catching Cindy Cooley in the hallway apparently returning from the washroom. He didn't have time to reassure her or even talk to her, so he just brushed past the startled, pale blonde. Gideon's murmur followed Lee into the room.

"It's okay, Cindy. Lee's intended just had a bit of a spell. We're going to let her lie down for a while."

Lee laid Genny on the bed, concerned that she'd actually fainted. Fainted! The woman could hire thugs to kill a man, but fainted on the front porch after hearing about a woman named Camille. Who'd have thought that would have sent her into a fit of vapors?

He brushed the curls away from her face and felt her forehead. Her skin was cool and clammy to the touch, her breathing a bit ragged.

"What do you need?" Gideon hovered in the doorway.

"Cool water, a cloth and quiet."

"Be right back." Gideon disappeared in a wink, leaving Lee with an unconscious Genny.

There weren't many things in life that frightened Lee. Not many he'd admit to anyway, but seeing Genny like this made him scared out of his wits. She was so strong, but maybe just tired. After all she worked really hard every day. Another horrible thought hit him—perhaps it was the rough sex in the mill. He hadn't intended on fucking her against the wall, but once they started, well, he didn't seem to be able to stop especially after the way she said Cornelius.

He stifled a hysterical laugh at the thought. Taking her in the mill was a stupid thing to do really and if it caused her harm, he'd never forgive himself. Gideon returned in moments with a pitcher, basin and a clean rag. He set them down on the floor beside the bed and poured the water into the basin to soak the cloth. Lee took the cloth from him and gently wiped her face.

Gideon left them alone while Lee wrestled with his own guilt. Perhaps he'd already ruined what had been gifted to him. Gabby poked her head in the door.

"Let me sit with her, Lee. Margaret's about to wear a hole in the front porch so you need to get downstairs and talk to her."

Lee looked down at Genny, so pale and small on the bed. Gabby put her hand on his shoulder. "It's okay, I'll take care of her, I promise."

With a reluctant nod, he stood and left the room, ready to find out just who this Camille was and what she wanted. He found Zeke, Jake and Gideon outside with Margaret.

"I'm going to the restaurant to find out what's going on. Will you come with me?" he asked Gideon.

"No need to even ask." Gideon was once again their captain. "Jake, you stay here with the women. Zeke, you come with us as sheriff of Tanger. We don't know what this woman's game is and I'd like the law there to witness whatever happens."

They split up, doing as he bade them. The three men walked in silence to the restaurant, Margaret trying to keep up with their long strides.

"If you'd slow down, I could catch my breath and tell you what I know." Margaret came to a stop and sucked in a lungful of air.

"I'm sorry." Gideon put his hand on her shoulder. "Matthew would have my hide if I did that in front of him. No need for your new husband to throw canned goods at my head."

Lee thought about what Gideon said. "Husband?"

"Yes, you fool. If you took your head out of your ass once in a while, you'd know that Matthew and Margaret got married four months ago." Zeke folded his arms across his chest and glared. "You've been hiding from the world at that mill for too long."

"Well I'm not hiding now, am I?" Lee snapped at him. "Don't you go judging me now, brother."

"I ain't judging you. You're just—"

"Stop it, both of you." Margaret huffed out an impatient breath. "Now I know we didn't part on the best of terms, Lee, but I wish you well with your new lady. I'm happy with my choice and I love him dearly. Now let's move on, okay?"

The three of them murmured their agreement while Lee really wanted to punch his brother.

"Now this woman came in about eight o'clock, not long ago, with a young man who isn't her husband, but he sure isn't her son. Good-looking fella with slicked back hair. They both had an accent, likely somewhere in Louisiana. It wasn't until they were halfway through supper when she asked me where Henry Blanchard lived." Margaret looked worried even in the gloom thrown by the houses around them. "I told her I wasn't sure, could she describe him and I'd go see what I could find. She's waiting on me to come back, just not with three walls of mean muscle."

"Louisiana? Are you sure?" According to Genny she was born and raised in New Orleans. His gut began to tighten with dread.

"Pretty sure. I knew a couple who were friends with my

Ben, back before the war. They were from Baton Rouge and had the same kind of lilting accent." Margaret took his hand. "I don't know what's going on, but if it involves your Genny, I'm willing to help in any way I can."

Lee pulled Margaret into an embrace, this time without a bit of the puppy love he'd had for her. "Thank you, Margaret. I can't tell you how much I appreciate it."

She stepped back with a small smile. "I can't believe you're the same man."

"Me either. I didn't get a hug," Zeke grumbled as he started walking. "Let's quit jawing and get walking to the restaurant."

"I'll hug you later," Gideon quipped.

Zeke growled at his cousin. "Shut up, Gid."

They walked the rest of the way to the restaurant in silence, the teasing jabs forgotten. Lee's throat felt parched as he stepped inside. He spotted the couple straight off, and he knew exactly who Camille was.

"Fuck," he said under his breath.

"Do you know her?" Zeke whispered.

"Not yet, but I know who she is."

Gideon and Zeke stood on either side of him as he made his way toward the strangers. The woman smiled at them with a sugary sweetness that made Lee's gorge rise. She had the same curly hair as Genny, her eyes were blue, and the heart shape of her face was mirrored in her granddaughter, Sophie.

This had to be Genny's mother.

"Gid, can you clear the restaurant?" he asked under his breath.

"On my way." Gideon spoke quietly to the few diners who were left, and Lee knew the restaurant would make no money that night.

Zeke stood in the corner near the table, arms folded, star clearly visible on his vest. Lee sat down, pleased he had a bit of an upper hand on her, and totally lost as to what to do to protect the woman he loved from the mother who'd sold her.

Camille looked around at the people being herded from the restaurant, then at Zeke. "Is there some kind of trouble, Sheriff?"

"Not yet."

Lee was never so glad his brother was a cold hard-ass of a sheriff. His brusque response rattled her, and Lee smiled inwardly at her discomfort.

"What do you want with Henry Blanchard?" he demanded.

"That's between me and Henry." She sipped at her drink which, judging by the scent, was tea laced with whiskey.

"No, that's between you and me."

She glanced up at him and raised one eyebrow. "I'm afraid I don't know you, *monsieur*. My name is Camille Boudreaux." Her gaze raked over his missing arm and he saw the distaste in her eyes. "Who are you?"

"Well, my name is Cornelius Blackwood, and I'm your daughter's new husband."

She started choking on the tea, and the young pup beside her slapped her on the back until she waved him away. Camille dabbed at her eyes with a lacy handkerchief. When she looked at Lee, this time the coquettish smile was gone and he saw the real woman she was. "*Merde*. That cannot be true."

"Oh it's true all right. Henry died in the spring and Genny married me today." No need to tell her they hadn't actually made it to the church yet. They'd become man and wife in heart and body, if not legally.

"And the child? Did the child survive?"

"What do you mean did the child survive? Did you never check on her after she left New Orleans?" Lee had never wanted to punch a woman before that moment.

"I could not. It would endanger her life. You see she had a hand in a man's death and that man's family was after her. She was pregnant and scared. I had to do what I could to protect her." Camille almost sounded sincere. "So I ask you again, did the child survive?"

Genny was pregnant before she came to Tanger? That meant Sophie was not Henry's child and had no claim to the farm at all. He began to understand why Genny was scared and reluctant to ask for help. Yet that didn't excuse what Camille did. "What the hell do you care? You sold your own daughter to that bastard Henry and left her to rot on that farm under his fists."

Camille raised one brow. "Is that what she told you? That I sold her?" She laughed without humor. "I'm afraid Genevieve has told you a falsehood. I did not take money for her. I paid Henry to take her and keep her safe, to save her life. When it was safe to bring her back to New Orleans, I told him I'd come to retrieve her."

Lee briefly considered the possibility Camille was telling the truth. What if Genny had misunderstood what her mother had done? He dismissed it immediately—he trusted his intended wife, and not this woman who pretended to be concerned about her.

"I don't believe you, Miss Boudreaux. Now take your man and leave Tanger and don't come back." He stood and glared down at the woman who'd given birth to Genny. "She won't want to see you."

Camille grabbed at his arm. "I am only concerned with my daughter and her child. What do I need to do to convince you?"

"You won't. Ever." He shook off her touch. "You can leave town the same way you came in. I won't allow you to hurt her anymore. Selling her to a man who beat her isn't even close to keeping her safe."

Lee nodded at Zeke and walked toward the door on shaky legs. Camille's voice shattered his control.

"*Mon dieu, monsieur.* I did not sell my daughter to a man who beat her. Henry was my cousin and he offered to take care of her. After all, what could I do with an incorrigible twelve-year-old?"

Genny woke with a start in a strange bed and an unfamiliar room. Her mouth was dry as dust and her head throbbed.

"It's okay, Genny." Gabby approached the bed from the corner of the room. She must have been sitting on the chair. "How are you feeling?"

Genny took a steadying breath. "I don't know. How did I get here?"

"You were outside with Lee, Gideon and Margaret. Then Lee came in with you in his arms pale as milk. He brought you upstairs then left to go to the restaurant." Gabby's dark eyes were full of worry. "I had to almost kick him out before he'd leave."

"Lee carried me upstairs?" She was trying to picture it.

"He had you partially on his shoulder, with your legs on his right arm. I don't know how he did it, but he's a different man than he was when he left here." Gabby shook her head. "Whatever you did was magic."

"I fainted?" She tried to sit up but dizziness assailed her.

"Yes, I think you did. I'm not sure why but if you like, I can ask Doctor Barham to come by." Gabby helped her into a sitting position.

"No, no need. I'm sure I'll be fine." She tried to remember what happened. "Did they say anything about why they were going to the restaurant?"

Gabby frowned and looked down at her hands.

"Please, tell me."

"Well, I don't know exactly, but Margaret said there was a woman at the restaurant who said her name was Camille and she was looking for Henry." Gabby's voice faded away, leaving Genny to try to suck in air.

Her head swam with the memory of hearing her mother's name again. She bent over and Gabby got the basin beneath her mouth before Genny vomited. Stars swam behind her eyes as she threw up all the fear, self-loathing and shame she'd been carrying for eight years.

Lee must already know more than Genny had revealed to him. Camille looked enough like her and Sophie for there to be an immediate connection. God, Genny wanted to curl up and die. Instead she put her face into the pillow and wept.

Gabby sat by her side, rubbing her back and murmuring soothing words. Genny had no idea how long she lay there feeling sorry for herself. She heard the men's voices downstairs and knew she couldn't hide any longer.

It was time to face her mother and the past she wanted to bury.

"Sounds like they're back." Genny sat up. "Can you give me a minute to wash my face?"

"Of course." Gabby tossed the dirty water from the basin out the window, then poured in fresh water from the pitcher. She pulled a clean rag from the washstand drawer and sat beside Genny.

Much to Genny's surprise, the other woman pulled her into a fierce hug. "I'm glad he found you. Please take care of him. He's not as tough as he seems."

With that, she left Genny alone to mull over her words and get herself ready to face her mother. She'd honestly thought the day would never come. Genny waited for years for her mother to arrive while figuring out how to take care of an infant when she was barely older than a child herself. Camille had broken so many promises, Genny hadn't really believed she'd come for her.

She'd been correct for eight years, until the day she asked Lee to marry her, the day her world was nearly perfect, and now the day she might have broken Lee's heart. Genny pressed the wet cloth into her swollen eyes, knowing there wasn't much she could do about it. Everyone would know she'd been crying and it wouldn't matter much anyway. Her mother's presence in Tanger would trump everything.

As she walked down the steps, Genny's stomach fluttered like there was a butterfly trapped inside. When she heard her mother's voice, she almost missed a step and barely stopped herself from falling head first. Perhaps breaking her neck would have been easier than seeing her mother again.

For years the memory of her last day in New Orleans played itself over and over in Genny's mind. She thought about it night and day until she almost lost her mind. When Sophie arrived she blessedly took over every moment in Genny's life, yet her dreams were never completely free. The memories of that dark day were rising up again, overwhelming her enough that she had to stop and sit on the steps for a minute.

Two weeks after she had been raped, Genny changed the course of her life for good. It had been raining earlier in the day so there was a mist rising from the streets. She had been dressed in the stableboy's clothes. They were scratchy but she was short enough to fit in them and pass for a boy. The coppery smell of blood was strong in the alley, along with piss, shit and moldering food.

She crouched behind some crates and watched as Allen Coddington lost his life. They stabbed him again and again, even after he collapsed to the ground. She knew they had to be sure he was dead, but when they slit his throat, she flinched and had to look away.

This was what she'd wanted, wasn't it? He'd brutally taken her virginity with whiskey on his breath and her protests ringing in his ears. Now his blood joined with hers and vengeance was taken. She wept silently into her hands as she listened to the two men wipe their knives on his clothes and walk away.

The alley was still except for the scrabbling of insects and rats nearby. Genny stood, her legs wobbly beneath her, and crept toward the body. He lay face up, the blood darker against his fancy silk vest. His mouth was open in a grimace of death, but it was his eyes that would haunt Genny. As she stood there, they moved until he stared directly at her.

That's when she turned and fled, heedless of where she was going. She sobbed as she ran, sorry for who she was, what she'd done. Once she stopped and vomited in another alley until there was nothing but bile coming up her throat. Then she continued on until she made it to the back door of her mother's house.

Bernard, the stableboy, was waiting for her. His eyes widened as he rose from the back steps. "You all right then, Genny?"

"No, I don't think I'll ever be right." She walked into the

carriage house and pulled off the clothes, ignoring Bernard's stare. Her small breasts were hidden by a cloth so he could only see her arms and feet. She yanked her dress off a hook in the tack room and pulled it on quickly.

Bernard stood in the corner watching her. "You've something on your shoes."

Genny glanced down and realized there was blood on her good leather boots. Mama would be furious with her for ruining them, but she sat down and yanked them off as quickly as she could.

"Thank you for your help, Bernard." She rose and handed the boots to him. "Burn them."

He nodded, wide-eyed, as she walked out of the stable barefoot, filthy and smelling of death and decay. She'd gone into the house and tried to wash up before her mother found her. By then Camille had heard of Allen's murder and slapped Genny so hard her ears rang.

"How dare you?" Camille had snarled. "You have no right to take revenge on an important man like that. Do you have any idea what they'll do to me if they find out?"

It was always about Camille, never about Genny. She let her mother rant and rave without saying a word. What could she say? Genny had become an adult and a murderess at the tender age of twelve.

A month later, Genny discovered she'd be a mother too. Her life, as pitiful as it was, had been destroyed completely. She thought it couldn't get any worse, but she'd been mistaken. Her mother found out about the pregnancy and rid herself of such a burdensome daughter.

Camille had shoved her into a carriage in the middle of the night with her awful cousin with the sweaty hands and smelly breath. "She's yours now, Henry. You know she's with child and out of control. She needs a firm hand, which I'm sure you won't mind. Do with her what you need to. I wash my hands of her for good." Camille turned and left Genny alone in the carriage with Henry without so much as a goodbye.

It was the last time she saw her mother. Genny rose to her feet and tried to swallow, but she had no spit left in her mouth. Jake appeared at the bottom of the steps and looked up at her. She couldn't hide any longer.

Chapter Nine

Genny stepped into the room slowly, Gabby at her heels. She saw her mother sitting at the table, a tall man behind her with dark chocolate hair and a bland expression. Although she didn't know him, he was as familiar as one of her mother's favorite hats—they all had the same style, they just looked slightly different. Same with her men.

"Hello, *Maman.*" Genny straightened her spine. "I never expected to see you again."

Her mother smiled and rose, arms outstretched. "Ah, *ma petite*, it's wonderful to see you. You look so tired." She brushed a kiss against each of Genny's cheeks as the familiar scent of Camille's perfume washed over her.

Genny closed her eyes against the waves of memories invoked by the simple scent. An ache spread in her chest and she had trouble catching her breath. She'd endured so much unhappiness, pain, darkness in her young life. Her mother was a monster with a pretty smile, one with an ugly side Genny knew too well. She stepped out of her mother's reach and walked over toward Lee, who stood near the sink, Sophie firmly attached to his leg.

His gaze was wary, but she also saw a little disappointment. She'd been honest with him for the most part. There were details she didn't quite tell him. He folded his hand around hers. Although she was still shaking, having him beside her helped her feel stronger.

"Why are you here, *Maman*?"

"*Ma petite*, I come to see you. Henry has kept you safe all these years from the Coddingtons. Now they have given up their search for you. The old man, Allen's father, died two weeks ago. No one is left to remember or seek vengeance."

Genny mulled over what her mother said, knowing of course she was probably lying. "Did you bring the clipping?"

Camille raised one brow. "Clipping?"

"Sirius Coddington's obituary clipping from the newspaper. That was his name."

Camille waved her hand as if shooing away a pesky fly. "Of course I brought no clipping. Why would I need one? You are my daughter. I tell you the truth as always." She smiled at Gabby, who stood silently in the doorway. "*Bonjour, Madame*. I am Camille Boudreaux and this is my traveling companion, Willard Hill."

Willard sketched a short bow while Camille held out her hands for Gabby. Bless her heart, Gabby had more fortitude than Genny did. She squeezed Camille's hands briefly.

"Hello, Miss Boudreaux. I am Gabrielle Sheridan. May I offer you some coffee?"

"How very polite you are. That would be wonderful." Camille sat down. "I have not had a good cup of coffee since I left New Orleans."

Gabby flashed a look at Lee who scowled fiercely at her. Genny understood though—Gabby was being a considerate hostess. Camille had done nothing to offend her and was wearing her polite social mask, which would likely slip when the others left the room.

"You did not answer my question, *Maman*. Why are you here?"

Camille waited until Gabby had set the cup of coffee in front of her. She didn't say a word, but she picked up the tin cup with two fingers as if it were the finest china. A backhanded insult to be sure. "I have come to visit you of course. This man here tells me Henry is dead."

Genny took a steadying breath. It had been so long since she'd played her mother's games, and she was sorely out of practice. Most folks in Tanger simply said what was on their minds, good or bad, blunt or sweet. Camille played a game of words. She was incredibly smart, very manipulative and devious as a demon.

"Henry died six months ago so you came for nothing. I have a farm to run and a daughter to raise." Genny was proud that her voice didn't tremble.

"Ah, *ma petite*, I didn't come for nothing. I came to see you, not Henry. Poor Henry, he was not young when he took you under his wing, but then we did what we could under the circumstances. I was lucky my cousin was in New Orleans when I needed him." Camille sipped at the coffee and pursed her lips as she swallowed, another subtle backhanded insult to Gabby.

"Henry didn't take me under his wing. He took me to his bed, he put me under his fists." Genny's voice grew stronger as she pushed aside her anger. "You are not welcome here so you can just pack up your Willard and go back to New Orleans."

Camille laughed at Genny's command. It was a tinkling, sing-songy laugh she'd practiced for years. It was a part of Genny's childhood, almost from the cradle. In fact, Genny couldn't remember a time she didn't hear it. Exactly as it sounded now, never different, never honest.

"You are too clever, Genevieve." Camille tutted at her. She cocked her head and pretended just to notice Sophie tucked behind Lee's leg. "This is the child, *oui*? Thank God she looks like me. Oh, but she needs pretty dresses and hair bows. She looks like a dirty street urchin."

"You'd better watch your mouth, lady, or my new daddy will kick your ass." Sophie frowned just as fiercely as her future stepfather did. For once, Genny was glad Sophie was outspoken.

"Your new daddy?" Camille's gaze raked up and down Lee, pausing on what was left of his shattered arm. "Ah yes, Mr. Blackwood told me of your nuptials. My felicitations. You'll be adopting the child then?" She said it so subtly, so nonchalantly, Genny had the awful thought that Sophie was the reason Camille had come to Tanger.

As his daughter, Sophie was the heir to Allen Coddington's fortune since he had no children prior to her birth. However, her life was here in Tanger, with Genny and Lee, no matter what Camille said or did.

"By law, Sophie is Henry's child, but Lee will adopt her." She glanced at him and he nodded ever so slightly. Genny felt a rush of emotion at the gesture and what it meant. Thank God he was willing to accept Sophie as his own. From what she could tell, the girl needed protection from her grandmother.

"I see. Well that's just wonderful." Camille's smile was too wide, too false. "I am glad I came to visit you. I can now get to know your daughter and your husband."

A shiver snaked up Genny's spine as she wondered exactly what her mother wanted and why.

Lee watched Genny confront her mother, her eyes red-rimmed and wide. After Camille's pronouncement she was there to get to know Sophie and Lee, Genny stood straighter as if she'd put on her battle armor.

"There is nothing for you here, *Maman*." Genny spoke through gritted teeth. "Since I'm no longer a child, you have no control over my child or what I do. I've already told you that you're not welcome here so leave."

Lee saw her shaking and knew it was costing Genny a lot to stand up to her mother. She was only twelve when Camille sent her away with Henry. It was the first time she confronted the woman who had sold her, abandoned her when she most needed a mother.

"Ah, *ma petite*, but this is not your home, *oui*? I have been welcomed by Mrs. Sheridan."

"No, it's not, but it belongs to my cousin." Lee finally spoke up. "You're here because I allowed it. As soon as you're done talking to Genny, you're gone."

"Genny? Hmm, why would you destroy such a beautiful French name? Genevieve, will you throw out your *maman* into the streets?" Camille was beautiful where Genny was plain, but damned if the older woman was dark where Genny was light.

God, he really did love her.

It was a hell of a time to accept it. He didn't want his emotions to cloud his judgment, considering Camille and her man posed a threat to all of them, regardless if she was Genny's mother.

"She doesn't need to." Lee stared at Genny until she looked at him. He nodded and he saw a shudder pass through her, hopefully one of relief. "I will make sure you leave the mill and Tanger. Since the hotel is closed and there's no boardinghouse, you've nowhere to stay the night."

Camille turned to him. Her cold stare sent a shiver up his spine, but he kept himself still as death. "Why would you be inhospitable to your mother-in-law, *Monsieur*? I am the only family Genny and Sophie have." She let loose the icy smile again.

"No, you're not. Genny is my wife and Sophie is my daughter."

"Yeah, he's my pa and I'll help him throw you into the street." Sophie really did need some discipline, but damned if Lee didn't want to hoot at the expression on Camille's face.

"The hostility in this room is simply ridiculous. I've come to spend time with my granddaughter and you're all treating me as if I'm the criminal here." She pinned her daughter with an accusing glance. "If Henry has died, it means you have no home unless your one-armed husband has one."

Genny frowned. "I have a farm, *Maman*. That is my home."

Camille laughed. "Oh, *ma petite*, you were not married to Henry therefore you have no claim on his farm. As his closest living relative, I do. It's perfect for us to visit, to become a family again." Her smile was wide and predatory.

"I lived with him for long enough to be his wife by law." Genny almost growled. Lee could see her vibrating with fury. "That farm is not yours. It's mine."

"Since you are not yet twenty-one, you cannot own the property. The farm is mine, *ma petite*." Camille straightened her shawl. "Come along, Willard. We'll be back in the morning to visit you at the farm. Be ready to receive us, Genevieve."

They left with the grace only the very well-to-do practiced. A moment of silence was broken by Genny's harsh breathing. She turned to Lee with a stricken expression on her face.

"I don't want her around Sophie."

"Yeah, I don't like her neither." Sophie wrapped her arms around both their legs, pulling them together.

Lee did the one thing he could think of—he held his ladies close and tried to figure out how to get rid of Camille Boudreaux. This was one fight he couldn't run away from.

Genny paced the kitchen like a caged creature, wringing her hands and mumbling to herself. She knew she looked like she'd lost all sense, but having her mother nearby left her breathless. Camille was heartless and twisted, so there was no telling what she was really there for. The possibilities were as numerous as they were dark.

Lee sat at the table with Jake, Zeke and Gideon. They talked quietly amongst themselves, but she could feel Lee watching her as she paced. He was worried about her. At least she hadn't lost him once he'd found out her secret. Being a mother at thirteen was nothing she was proud of, particularly considering Sophie had been a child of rape. A child who became the light of love, the very reason for Genny to live. She'd gone upstairs to rest, thank God. She didn't have to witness the aftermath of her grandmother's visit.

The jubilant mood had been crushed flat by the arrival of Camille. Where there had been celebration, laughing and smiling, now the group was somber, worried and confused. Gabby and Naomi sipped tea while the men put drops of whiskey in their coffee, all but Zeke anyway. He didn't drink anything at all.

The tension in the room had grown. It was as if the world that Genny had come to know had been torn in half and turned inside out. The last person she ever expected to see was her mother, certainly not on the day that she had proposed to the man she loved. The men seemed to be looking to Zeke and Gideon. She knew they'd been in the war together and Gideon had been their captain. Zeke had obviously been the type of soldier to get them out of a tight situation, a thinker, a strategist.

Genny decided she might as well speak because she was sure they were trying to find a delicate way to let her know her mother was a manipulative bitch.

"This is how I see things," she began. "As you know, I came to Tanger with Henry while I was pregnant by another man. She sold me, to be truthful." She took a deep breath before continuing. Discussing her pitiful past was harder than she thought. "There's no love lost between my mother and I. I was more of an inconvenience to her, although I was one of the many reasons that my father kept her in a fancy house in her silk clothes and servants, with chocolate each morning. Camille uses anyone and everything that she can. Do not believe what she tells you. She knows how to twist words, hide facts, tell half-truths until you're unsure if your head is on your shoulders or sticking out your rear end."

Gideon watched her with his kind blue eyes. She decided she liked this cousin of Lee's. He exuded a calmness that affected everyone. It was no wonder he'd been their leader. "What does your mother really want?"

Genny took Lee's hand. "I don't know and that scares me more than anything. My mother is capable of a lot."

"Don't worry, honey. We're all here for you." Lee tucked her beneath his arm and she felt protected if only for a moment.

"She has no idea how stubborn Blackwoods are." Zeke's smile was positively feral.

Genny managed a small smile. "Thank you. Thank you very much, Zeke. The other part of this," Genny continued, "has to do with Sophie. Her father was Allen Coddington, one of New Orleans' most eligible bachelors. In the eyes of the law however, she is Henry's daughter. I don't know what my mother's plans are, but I can't let her stay here. I can't let her take over my life or God forbid, Sophie's. Camille's first and only thought is for herself. She must not get near Sophie again."

The conviction, the iron in Genny's voice as the strength grew within her, made her spine straighter, made her words sharper. All the men nodded.

"I can see that," Zeke said. "I've dealt with women who are less than upstanding citizens before. Most of us have."

They all shared a look and Genny wondered how she'd found such an amazing family to fall into.

"What did she mean about the Coddingtons not being a threat anymore?" Zeke cut to the heart of it.

Genny inwardly winced. "His family has a lot of influence, and a lot of money. After Allen was killed, Camille told me his family would want me dead. I don't know if she's telling the truth about his father's death though."

"We can send a wire to New Orleans in the morning and find out," Zeke piped up. "It could be from me—the sheriff's office wouldn't raise any suspicions—without mentioning you at all."

"So what do we do while we wait?" Lee looked at Gideon first, then at Zeke. "If she really is the owner of the farm by law, we can't keep her off the property. I'm pretty sure that woman is not going to give up whatever she's after very easily."

Genny's blood ran cold at the thought. Lee was right—Camille didn't let anything stand in her way, ever.

Gideon looked at Genny. "I'd say the first step..." he glanced at Lee, "...is to get the two of you hitched as soon as possible."

The mention of marrying Lee set a tumble of joy inside her that warred with the worry, anxiety and anger she was struggling with. She took Lee's hand and squeezed. "I'm ready."

Lee cleared his throat before he looked up at Gideon then at Genny. "I'm ready too. After we get hitched, how do we get rid of her? What if she's right and Genny has no claim to the farm?"

The truth was, Genny was fairly certain Camille was right about the farm. She didn't want the farm, she wanted Sophie. If it came down to a choice between them, there was no choice. Genny would rather live off the charity of others. She'd do just about anything to survive if it meant keeping Sophie safe and away from Camille.

"That's going to take some more thinking. It's also going to take some help." Gideon looked at Zeke. "In the morning after you wire about this Coddington fella, wire Nate to see if he could help."

Everyone nodded. Genny had heard mention of Nate, but didn't know how he could help her now. Yet anyone who could offer assistance was welcome.

Zeke offered an explanation. "Nate lives over in Grayton with his wife Elisa. After he settled there, he took some schooling and became a lawyer. His wife runs the ranch and he runs a law practice. He can help us. Nate's going to ask some tough questions. He's going to keep your secrets safe unless he needs them to do what he needs to do to help you."

Genny nodded, swallowing hard. "I'm sure that he's trustworthy, especially if he's a friend of y'alls." Judging by their expressions, they all thought very highly of Nate.

Gideon pointed at Lee. "You and Genny get over to the church and wake Gregory to get hitched tonight. Jake and Gabby, you go with them as witnesses."

Genny's mouth dropped open. "Tonight? I thought you meant tomorrow, but tonight?"

"You said you were ready." Gideon frowned.

"I'm ready, but Sophie's asleep." She didn't want to get married without her daughter there, but waking her at midnight wouldn't make for a very happy child at a wedding. It had been a rough enough day for everyone.

"We can have a great big wedding afterwards and invite the whole town. Tonight it will be just the four of you. We'll work out the rest of it later." Gideon looked at Zeke. "I'll stay here with Naomi and keep an eye on the girl. You do a perimeter search and make sure everything is secure. We'll take turns keeping watch until they get back."

Gideon was definitely used to being in charge and giving orders. Right about then, Genny wasn't about to argue with him. She took Lee's hand and kissed him hard. "Let's go get married."

The last thing Lee expected to be doing that night was getting married and figuring out how to get rid of his future mother-in-law. Hell, he hadn't even been engaged the day before. They walked to the church in silence, Genny's hand firmly tucked into his. It seemed life was trying to tell him something and he was finally listening. He'd been offered a gift, and he'd be a fool and a half if he didn't accept it.

Jake held Gabby's elbow, carefully helping her step over anything that was bigger than a pebble. She chuckled over his attentiveness, but it was apparent to everyone she enjoyed the attention. The love, the tenderness, the sheer joy he saw between them actually made him wish for it himself, rather than wish it away.

He stumbled at the thought of seeing Genny round with his child, *their* child. The dusty ground rushed toward him, then Genny caught his arm, stopping his fall. Thankfully she said nothing about his clumsiness.

Yet the image of her pregnant was now permanently etched in his mind. Normally he would have run, literally, from anything to do with children or marriage. Now here he was on his way to wake up the preacher and get hitched, and he had a seven-year-old daughter who would be his responsibility in about twenty minutes.

Why wasn't he running the opposite direction? What was it about this woman and her child that made him want to stand still and put down roots? Maybe it was like Zeke told him, love hits between the eyes and there ain't no way to stop it.

The streets of Tanger were quiet so late at night. The only sounds were the night creatures singing to each other and the whisper of a breeze on the leaves of the trees. The four of them arrived at the church in ten minutes and as suspected, everything was dark. Lee remembered fixing the roof of the church with Zeke right after they'd first arrived in Tanger, but he also remembered the preacher and his daughter who lived there had been murdered by the very marauders the Devils had been hired to stop. Life in Tanger had been bloody and unpredictable, now it was just maddening and unpredictable.

They walked around to the small rectory house and knocked on the door. Lee had to knock two more times before he finally heard a voice from within.

"I'm coming, just give me a moment." It was muffled, but the voice definitely belonged to Gregory Conley, the young minister who'd arrived in Tanger the year before. He'd brought back not only regular Sunday service but more enthusiasm than a body ought to even have. Although the permanent smile on Gregory's face could be annoying, Lee liked him and was glad he'd settled in town.

A warm glow appeared inside, visible through the window.

The door opened and Gregory stood there barefoot in a pair of trousers with his shirt unbuttoned and his short dark hair mussed by sleep. He held up the lamp and looked at all of them.

"Good evening, Jake, Lee, oh and Mrs. Sheridan and another lady." His cheeks colored in embarrassment. "Please come in."

Without asking them any questions, he opened the door wide and ushered them in. He put the lantern on the table and buttoned up his shirt, keeping his gaze on the floor. Lee wanted to tell the boy not to be embarrassed then thought better of it. A preacher didn't usually show off his chest to his congregation's female members.

Jake wasted no time. "Greg, we need your help."

"Of course, anything." He looked a little bewildered and not quite awake.

Lee nodded to Genny. "This is Genevieve Blanchard. She and I are fixing to get hitched. This may be the first midnight wedding you perform, but we need you to marry us. Now."

Greg looked back and forth between them, surprise clearly written on his face. "You are getting married?" He and the preacher had never been close, but he didn't need to act as if Lee had sprouted two heads.

"I know I ain't as good-looking as Zeke or as charming as Jake, and not to mention I'm missing an arm, but yep, I'm getting married." Saying it out loud made his stomach do a dance the likes of which he'd never experienced. Holy ever-loving shit.

He was getting married.

Greg smiled, held out his hand to Genny and squeezed hers briefly. "It's wonderful to meet you, Genevieve. I must say I never expected Lee to settle down but I couldn't be happier." He glanced between Lee and Jake. "Wait a minute, you said you wanted me to perform the ceremony now?"

"I can't get into the details but you know we wouldn't wake you up if we didn't need to do this tonight. Lee and Genny were already engaged so we're just hurrying the ceremony along." Jake gestured to Greg's clothes. "We don't need your accoutrements but if you want to change, now is the time."

Greg glanced down. "I, uh, would feel more comfortable wearing the collar. I'll only be a few minutes. Why don't you go to the church and I'll meet you there?" He disappeared into the gloom without waiting for an answer.

Jake lit another lantern that sat on the table and led them back out of the house to the church. Genny was quiet, too quiet, and Lee knew she was worrying about Sophie. He didn't blame her because when he wasn't marveling over the fact he'd have a wife in ten minutes, Lee was worrying about the brat too.

That mother of Genny's was hiding behind a pretty face and fancy clothes. He couldn't imagine growing up with a mother who had been a rich man's plaything, a woman who apparently only kept her daughter to control the rich man. His own mother had had a good heart even if she'd smothered him. Camille was a monster, or maybe a dragon they needed to slay.

Although he didn't plan on killing the woman, he wasn't above it if it meant protecting Genny and Sophie. The very thought of losing one of them would be enough to make him do anything he needed to.

He hadn't spent much time wondering what his wedding would be like. That's something young women did, not a war veteran who'd lost all his dreams long ago. Yet when they walked into the church, he was awash in the memories of the weddings he had attended, including Jake's and Zeke's.

The flowers in the ladies' hair, the smiling grooms, the

neighbors, the celebration and the pure joy flowing through everyone. He'd been happy for them, but at the same time he'd been envious. An ache had settled in his chest when he'd watched his brother and his friend marry the women they loved.

Now looking toward the front of the church illuminated by only the lantern, he realized he'd be standing up marrying the woman he loved.

A lump grew in his throat and he coughed to cover his embarrassment. His friends might tell him there was nothing to be embarrassed about, but that didn't make a lick of difference. He was feeling things he hadn't felt for a very long time. He'd been swimming in dark emotions and now the brightness of Genny shone into the shadows of his heart.

Lee and Genny walked slowly toward the front, each of them quiet, perhaps lost in thought. Her hand tightened in his as they reached the pulpit. She looked up at him, her eyes glittering in the lamplight. Her hair was like a frizzy halo around her, the curls long since escaped from the bun she'd twisted that morning.

"A midnight wedding." She shook her head. "A story to tell our grandchildren."

Lee nodded, his throat still too tight to speak. Gabby pulled Genny to the side and started to fuss with the bride's hair.

"Let's see if we can fix this a bit." Gabby towered over the smaller woman, but there was so much emotion in the air, and Gabby was so gentle, they seemed to be more like sisters than friends.

Jake put a hand on his shoulder. "This is a big surprise."

"Truer words were never spoken." Lee watched Genny as she prepared for their wedding. He wanted to give her something more, but he didn't even have a wedding band, for God's sake.

178

"Zeke gave me something for you." Jake pulled a small cloth from his shirt pocket. "He said it was too small for Naomi, but that Genny was tiny enough it might work."

Jake unfolded the light-colored cloth to reveal a gold band. Lee's heart pounded at the sight of the ring—the marriage was that much more real to him. He picked up the ring with fingers that trembled only a bit. It winked in the meager light, and Lee realized exactly where his brother had gotten the ring.

"It was my mother's. I didn't know he had it." Lee remembered saying goodbye to their mother before the war. It was the last time they'd seen her; sometime during the years they were away, she'd died. Lee hadn't even told her he loved her or given her a kiss goodbye. He'd been such an ass for so long, he was surprised Genny could see beneath the layers of shit built up around him.

He'd hated his mother's smothering, her constant fussing, and did all he could to put as much space between them as possible. Now she was gone and the only thing left of her was the cool band in his palm. She must have given Zeke things he could sell if they'd needed money. Even from heaven, she was reaching down to take care of Lee, her baby boy. He tucked the ring into his pocket, warmed by the idea of having a piece of her love.

The door to the church opened and Gregory came in, lantern in one hand, Bible in the other and preacher's collar firmly around his neck. He smiled at them as he walked toward the pulpit.

"I'm sorry to have taken so long. I wanted to wash the sleep off my face." The minister set the lantern on the pulpit and turned to face them. "Are you ready?"

Lee's gaze snapped to Genny's and when she smiled, he knew they were doing the right thing. This was what God had in mind all along. He just had to find his way through the darkness to her light.

"Ready." Lee held out his hand and Genny took it. Her palm was warm and small, fitting snugly inside his. Even if traditionally the bride stood on the left, she settled on the right so they could remain holding hands.

When they turned to face the minister, all doubt and fear were gone. The ceremony was short and before Lee realized they'd started, Jake was nudging him.

"The ring, Lee."

"What? Oh, the ring." He let go of her hand and fumbled in his pocket.

"You have a ring?" Genny sounded as surprised as he'd been when Jake had shown it to Lee.

"You have a ring?" the minister repeated. "That's wonderful."

As Lee slid the ring onto Genny's finger, everything he thought was missing from the wedding suddenly was clear to him. Joy suffused him as the ring fit perfectly onto her slender finger. She looked up at him with a sheen of tears in her eyes.

Love had finally found its way into Lee Blackwood's dark heart.

Chapter Ten

It was dark as pitch, but Gideon wanted it that way. He stood near the kitchen table, as silent as a single breath.

Someone was in the mill.

He'd been drinking coffee in the dark when the first noises began. Small, scratching sounds near the door had him on his feet, pistol in each hand. Then came a shuffling, likely shoes on the dirt on the wooden floor.

Zeke hadn't come back yet, so Gideon was alone to defend Sophie, Naomi, Cindy Cooley and Gabby's invalid father, Sam. Not very good odds, but luckily they were all upstairs sleeping. He could focus better without any distractions.

He hoped the rest of them made it back from the church soon, but in the meantime, he had to focus on the noises. Whoever it was crept closer to the kitchen and the stairs which gave access to the second floor. Gideon had to stop them no matter what and he knew it.

It had been years since he'd been on a battlefield but the truth was, once a soldier, always a soldier. His hands tightened on the grips as the shuffling grew nearer. Gideon breathed in slow and shallow, even as his heart beat a steady tattoo.

A movement in front of him startled him, a shadow even darker than that which surrounded him. Gideon strained to see where it moved, but he lost it in the room. If the stranger got upstairs, Gid would have failed at his task to protect his family and that was simply unacceptable.

He considered his options within seconds. The stairs were to his right, the most vulnerable spot in the room. Once he moved the shadow would know he was there and he'd lose his advantage. However, since he had no idea where the stranger was, he had to do something.

Being a leader meant making hard decisions, ones that put him and others in danger, sometimes mortal danger. In this instance, he really didn't have a choice. He wasn't a hero, he was simply doing what he was meant to do.

Gideon let out a rebel yell and ran toward the stairs.

As they walked back to the mill, Genny felt dazed. She'd finally gotten married, her first real wedding, and it had taken place by lantern light at midnight in a small, quiet church. It was an odd ceremony, to be sure, but nevertheless, it had been the one thing in her life, aside from Sophie, that felt absolutely right.

She held Lee's hand, the ring heavy on her finger. Genny had never had jewelry so it felt odd to have something so permanent. She wanted to ask him where he'd gotten the ring, but was afraid to. Perhaps it was meant for another woman before the war, before he'd lost his arm. She really didn't want to know, but later on, after the situation with her mother was over, she might ask.

Lee stopped and tugged on her hand. "The mill is dark."

Gabby and Jake stopped beside them. All four studied the side of the building, searching for some sign of life. Genny's stomach flipped when she realized Lee was right. The mill was completely dark, without a flicker of light anywhere. It could mean everyone was asleep, which she knew was not likely. Zeke and Gideon were watching over Sophie for her.

Fear roared through her at the threat to her daughter. She knew Camille had ulterior motives for her visit—dark motives that could only bode ill for everyone. Genny started running for the mill, her heart in her throat. She heard Lee curse then the sound of footsteps running behind her. It didn't matter that he was the man and the protector. Nothing mattered but her little girl.

"Sophie!" Her daughter's name was torn from her throat as she ran faster than she'd ever done, faster than the wind, faster than the frantic beating of her heart.

Almost in response to her shout, a howl came from within the dark building.

"Jesus fucking Christ, that's Gideon!" Lee was suddenly beside her, giving her an extra boost to run the last hundred yards.

A gunshot echoed in the night, followed by a scream. Lee passed her and slammed into the mill, rolling into a crouch as he did. Jake shoved her aside and went inside after Lee using the same method. Genny stumbled up the steps, Gabby close on her heels.

"Wait, Genny!" She grabbed her ankle. "Let them do what they do best. If you go in there, you might get hurt instead of whoever needs to be."

Genny tried to shake off her new friend's grip. "I can't stay out here. That's my daughter in there." Her voice ended on a sob as she struggled with the panic that clawed its way up her spine. "Please, Gabby, let me go."

Gabby was bigger and stronger and she kept a firm grip on Genny's leg, no matter how much she struggled. Another howl resonated into the darkness, along with sounds of a struggle, grunts and more cursing from at least three different voices.

Genny's tears streamed down her face as she called Sophie's name, absolute terror mixing with fury in her soul.

"You need to shut up." Zeke appeared on the steps next to her, his face a mask of stone and fury. "Your caterwauling is going to get them killed. Don't distract a man when he's in battle, Mrs. Blackwood, or you'll get your new husband killed." He took her arm and held on firmly. "They're fighting for their lives in there. Do you understand me?"

Genny managed to nod although she was almost as frightened for Lee now as she was for Sophie. She never even considered the men's lives were in danger. How had things become such a mess?

"I'm sorry," she whispered. "I'm so scared."

Zeke loosened his grip. "So am I, but if I go in there now they're liable to shoot me. I have to sit out here and listen to them, knowing my entire family is in there with their lives on the line. If something happens to you two, Lee and Jake will never forgive me."

Beneath the hard mask of his expression, Genny saw the fear and love Zeke obviously didn't express often. He was the most aloof of the Devils she'd met and marveled that Naomi was able to chip away at the ice covering him. Zeke cared deeply, perhaps so deeply others couldn't see how much.

"I'm sorry," she repeated. "I didn't know what my mother would—"

He cut her off. "Your mother's actions are not yours. Lee loves you and that means you're family too. We take care of our own."

With that, Genny sat beside her new brother-in-law, confused and scared out of her wits as she listened to her husband fight for his life and her daughter's safety.

Lee knew exactly where Jake was, but the two figures rolling around on the floor included Gideon. He couldn't tell which one was Gid and couldn't see an opening to break them apart. Jake crouched near the steps, hissing up at whoever was there to stay upstairs.

He had to do something and fast. Someone might have been wounded by the shot he'd heard. All the cold nights, the fear, the taste of battle, came rushing back at him. Lee knew what he had to do. He stood up, let loose the rebel yell he'd perfected and jumped into the fray.

He recognized Gideon's form in the darkness. A dark form had his cousin by the neck, choking the life from him. Lee punched the stranger in the kidneys, but the man didn't let loose. Sweet fury controlled him as he used his fingers like claws on the man's face, aiming for his eyes. Teeth cut into his hands and Lee cursed loudly.

"Fucking bastard!" He let the man's arm go, slid around behind him and yanked the man's slick hair as hard as he could. Lee felt the hair rend from the scalp and the warmth of blood seep onto his hand. He kicked at an elbow, then he heard rather than felt Gideon cough as he rolled to the side.

Thank God he'd gotten free. Lee twisted the head of hair, but it was so greasy it slipped right through his fingers. A knee came down on his balls and pain exploded through him. He fought the urge to vomit as the stranger continued to kick him. Lee made a blind grab for the man's foot but only grazed his pant leg.

Lee couldn't get a breath in to say anything so he was surprised when the attack stopped. Heavy breathing filled the dark room along with the sound of something dripping.

"Whoever you are..." Gideon's raw voice came from his left, "...we'll kill you before you get your hands on the girl. Your choice is to leave now or leave in a pine box."

There was no response, but Lee heard a swooshing noise and a groan of pain that made the hairs on the back of his neck stand up.

"Shoot him." The voice sounded like Gideon, but it was unlike anything he'd ever heard. Whatever happened, Gid was most definitely not okay.

A flash and boom of a gun was the only warning that Gideon's command had been heard. The shot came from the stairs, which meant it was Jake. Someone fell to the floor with an audible thump to Lee's right. He felt a measure of satisfaction that Jake had gotten the lousy son of a bitch.

"Light, we need light," Jake shouted.

Lee tried to stand but found he could only get to his knees since his hand was still cupping the throbbing stones between his legs.

Lantern light filled the room and Lee glanced around to see the man who'd come into the mill with Camille, Willard his name was, lying sightless on the floor, a pool of blood beneath him. Damn, they'd been right all along about her. She'd sent her male whore to steal the granddaughter she'd never even seen before that day. The woman was more devious than any person he'd ever met.

"Gid, oh my God, Gid." Jake knelt next to Gideon. Blood coated their captain's light blue shirt. "That bastard stabbed him."

Lee crawled over, the coppery tang of blood growing stronger as he got to Gideon's supine form. Jake pulled off his shirt and pressed it into Gideon's chest. Tears of rage filled the redhead's eyes.

Gideon's blue eyes were a haze of pain and confusion. Blood seeped from the corner of his mouth and his throat was a mass of reddened skin where he'd been choked. What had Lee brought upon his family? While he was out getting married and thinking happy thoughts, an intruder had tried to kill the people he loved.

"We need the doc, Lee," Jake shouted at him. "Dammit, get up and do something."

No matter the pain from the groin kick, Lee got to his feet and ran out the door. He saw Zeke crouched with Genny and Gabby near the stairs, but he didn't stop.

"Doc," was all he managed to get out.

Every second Gideon's life was ticking away. There was no time to waste.

Gabby was the first to go into the house yelling Jake's name. Genny stared after Lee. He'd had blood on his hands and shirt, and a look of pure desperation on his face. He must be going to Doctor Barham's house, which meant someone inside was hurt.

Zeke was the next into the mill, leaving Genny to drag herself up. Her fear had become self-loathing over what had happened. She'd spent most of her life believing she had been a mistake, a person who was never meant to be. Giving birth to Sophie, finding love with Lee, had pulled her from the depths of human excrement.

Now she was right back in there, knowing she was responsible for whatever had happened inside that mill. She'd caused pain and suffering for Lee's family because her mother was evil incarnate. Genny could ask why over and over, but no answer would ever come. Life had not been too kind to the illegitimate piece of white trash pretending to be an everyday farm wife. Why would it change now?

When she screwed up her courage to go into the mill, the

smell of blood hit her first. Her gorge rose, as did the vivid memory of standing over Allen's body in the alley. She swallowed down the bile that threatened and looked around at the destruction.

The tables and chairs were either knocked over or broken. Gabby was on her knees at Gideon's head while Jake and Zeke were like bookends beside him. Gabby had helped the doctor with nursing over the years and thank God she had. Naomi was tearing sheets and handing them to Gabby to stem the bleeding in Gideon's chest.

Jake's wife looked up. "Genny, get some water boiling."

Genny ran to the stove, grateful for something to do. As she stoked up the fire, she noticed another body lay on the floor near the stairs. It was Willard, Camille's newest toy. Genny trembled with the absolute certainty that her presence may have caused Gideon's death.

"Don't faint on me now, Genevieve," Zeke barked. "I told you this wasn't your fault. Now get your ass moving and boil water so Gabby can save his life."

Genny nodded, too scrambled to do anything else. She watched as Zeke and Jake picked Gideon off the floor and onto a blanket Naomi had put on the table. Gideon groaned in pain and a sob burst from somewhere to Genny's left.

She looked over to see a slender blonde woman standing in the shadows. Her hand covered her mouth as her blue eyes welled with tears. Genny had no idea who the woman was, but she was doing what Genny couldn't. If she let the tears loose, there'd be no stopping them. No, she had to be strong, she had to do something to save this man who had protected her daughter.

"Where's Sophie?" Genny suddenly realized there was one person not present.

"Cindy, is the girl still asleep upstairs?" Jake asked the blonde.

She nodded and put her palms together, pressing them against her cheek with her head cocked. Sleeping. She was saying Sophie was sleeping.

Genny went over to the sink to pump water into the bucket as the fire grew hotter. She managed to catch the woman's gaze. "Thank you."

The blonde shook her head and pointed at Gideon. Genny wondered if there was a relationship between the strangely quiet woman and Gideon, but now wasn't the time to ask. She put the bucket on the stove and grabbed another.

Naomi came over and opened the hot water reservoir, ladling out the last of it into a bowl. "Put some fresh water in here too, Genny. We'll need as much hot water as we can get I think."

The next ten minutes were a blur as Genny filled two more buckets and started on a fourth. Her arms were screaming in agony from pumping the water so hard and carrying what was probably forty pound buckets to the stove. It didn't matter though, not one little bit. None of it mattered if Gideon was dying.

Lee burst into the mill, a frazzled-looking Dr. Barham in tow. Genny looked at her new husband and felt the depth of his agony over Gideon's dire wounds. She wanted to pull Lee into her arms and weep with him. She sucked back the weakness of her own grief and kept her focus on helping.

"Everyone but Gabby, stand back." He set his bag on a chair. "Tell me what's happened."

"He was stabbed twice, once below the ribs and the other right through the fifth and sixth ribs on the right side." Gabby spoke cleanly and crisply, focusing on the job, no doubt, instead of the copious amounts of blood on the bandages. "I think it missed the lungs, but there might be organ damage. I've slowed the bleeding, but he'll need to be stitched immediately."

"I assume the gentleman on the floor doesn't need my help." Doctor Barham waited for Gabby's confirmation before continuing. "Good, then where's the hot water?"

Everyone turned to look at Genny. She felt their pain, their worry and pushed her guilt aside. "The first bucket is ready."

Naomi brought her a clean bowl, and Genny ladled in piping hot water with shaking hands. It would be the first of many that night.

As the doctor ripped open Gideon's shirt, he shooed the men out of the room. "Go outside and pace. You'll only distract us."

Genny would stay and help all she could. While Naomi ran back and forth for water, more bandages and whatever Gabby and the doctor needed, Genny kept the water boiling for the next two hours. The surgery was gruesome and gave Genny an appreciation for what doctors do. As she stood guard over the water, deep down all she could do was pray that Gideon would survive.

If he didn't, she knew her marriage was over before it had begun.

After washing off his hand in the river, Lee wrapped a handkerchief around the bite marks from the bastard Willard. The remaining three Devils were gathered in back near the wheel, their favorite spot to talk and think out loud. The man lying on the table inside should have been there with them, but God willing, he would join them the next time.

"That mother-in-law of yours is a fucking bitch." Zeke stood with his hands on his hips, glaring at no one in particular.

190

"Genny warned us Camille was up to something. Now we know what. Fucking bitch is a kind way to describe her." Jake sat on the stone wall, a piece of grass in his mouth. "I can't believe that sweet woman in there came from that vicious cunt."

Lee walked over to Jake and held out his hand. "Tie this, would you?" He was surprised to find he felt no embarrassment about asking for help tying. Used to be he'd use his teeth and anything else he could to avoid asking for help. The expression on Jake's face confirmed he was just as shocked.

As Jake tied off the bandage, he frowned at Lee. "You saved him, you know? I couldn't figure out who was who in the dark."

Lee sat next to his friend. "I don't know if I saved him or not. Willard was choking Gideon, so I just beat at the bastard until he let go. Maybe if I'd just shot him, Gid wouldn't be in there bleeding to death." Guilt was a familiar companion for most soldiers, and he'd had his fair share of what ifs.

"That's a load of horse shit." Jake looked at Zeke. "Lee jumped in there like a wildcat, as always, and the bad guy ended up dead. Sometimes your brother's antics are for good instead of evil."

"That true? He was choking Gid and you stopped him?" Zeke peered at Lee with that intense stare of his.

"I did what I had to. Bastard bit me but I pulled off half his scalp, then he kicked me in the balls." Which were currently still aching and probably would for at least another hour. Nice wedding night this had turned out to be. "Jake here shot the son of a bitch dead, not me."

"How the hell did you manage not to kill the wrong person?" Zeke sat on the other side of Jake. Lee could almost see his brother shaking with the need to go find Camille and strangle her.

"I am a crack shot." Jake raised one brow. "And I knew Lee

191

was down judging by the groans, and Gideon was definitely on the floor. That left the only person standing the one I needed to shoot."

Zeke nodded. "Good thing your aim was true, Sergeant, or I would have blown his head clear off his body if he had come out that door."

Lee's anger was always hotter than the sun, burning so fast and fierce he usually didn't have a moment to think before he acted. Zeke's was more like a smoldering vat of embers, ones that would kill you before you even realized how hot they were. In that respect, they were different as could be, but the need for revenge was a different story.

"We're going to go find her, right?" Lee asked.

"Damn straight. That bitch is mine." Zeke patted his pistol as if making sure it was still strapped to his thigh.

"I hope you mean to arrest her and not shoot her." Jake was the calmest of the three. "Ain't no way that idiot Willard broke into the mill on his own. She was behind it and she needs to be arrested and put on trial for attempted murder and kidnapping."

Zeke plucked at his badge. "I don't know if I can do that. Right about now all I want to do is see her blood on the wall behind her."

Lee tasted the same need for vengeance. That woman had put her own greed above human life, and when those lives were his family, there was no way he'd let her get away with it. The only thing holding him back was Genny.

It seemed like days ago they stood in front of Gregory and said their I dos to become man and wife. The memory was bittersweet considering the violence and death that had followed.

"We need to bunker down for a few days." Jake,

unbelievably, was the voice of reason in Gideon's absence. He was usually the Devil looking for the backdoor way to get things done, not the most logical. "Let her know she didn't beat us, that we're all standing guard over Sophie. Gideon can heal while we figure out what the hell to do with this woman and her threat."

Lee hadn't spoken to Genny since the attack, since he'd almost lost one of the four men who were closest to him in the world. As quiet settled over the group, he thought about exactly how he did feel. He knew it wasn't Genny's fault and she was more surprised than he was to see her mother in Tanger.

God, he definitely loved her, just the thought of holding her made goose bumps march down his skin. Genny was a flower in the middle of a manure pile, and he was the lucky son of a bitch who got to call her wife. If she lost the farm, possible considering she never had legal control over it, they'd have to find somewhere else to live. Hell, maybe it was time he really did become an accountant and support his new family.

"She's not to blame, you know." Zeke's quiet words were loud in the night air.

"No, not at all. Genny is an angel and has always been good folk. She couldn't choose her parents any more than I could." Jake's crooked smile hid the pain of being illegitimate himself, a bastard Blackwood never acknowledged by the once mighty family.

Lee was grateful for their acceptance of Genny's innocence in the debacle that just occurred. Now he would probably have to convince her of that fact. Judging by the way she looked at him earlier, guilt had already thrown its shroud over her heart.

Chapter Eleven

Her eyes felt as if someone had poured sand in them. Genny rubbed at them, knowing they would only hurt more but unable to stop herself. It had been one of the longest nights of her life, wondering if Gideon would survive. The doctor was amazing, as were Gabby's nursing skills. Genny would trust her life to either one of them.

While the women stayed in the kitchen, keeping watch over Gideon, the men patrolled the outside of the mill. They'd gotten rid of Willard's body right after the doctor had arrived, thank God.

The mill felt like a fort with soldiers watching over them. In a way, it was, although Genny didn't like the feeling one bit. Thankfully Gideon didn't get a fever and he seemed to be resting comfortably.

She had to talk to Lee, see him, touch him, kiss him, if only to reaffirm life and their love for each other. After murmuring to Naomi and Gabby that she'd be back in a few minutes, Genny went out onto the porch. The muted light of dawn painted everything an eerie shade of gray. It looked lifeless and gloomy outside.

Jake was on the front porch, shotgun cradled in his arms. He gestured to the side of the mill and she smiled at him in thanks. Genny stepped onto the grass, the dew immediately washing her feet and ankles. Her shoes had been nearly ruined with the night's activities so she'd left them to dry by the stove, hopeful the blood would come out of the leather.

Lee stood on the low stone wall, pistol strapped to his thigh, and hat pulled low on his forehead. He spotted her immediately and jumped down. Genny couldn't stop herself if she tried. She ran toward him and when he opened his arm wide, a sob burst from her throat.

She burrowed into his warmth, her tears soaking the collar of his shirt. He didn't say anything, but he held her tight and let her cry until her inner storm had passed. Genny pulled a handkerchief from her skirt pocket and blotted her eyes, then blew her nose. She let out a honk that made Lee snort.

"Are you okay?" She finally looked at him and saw the love on his face. Love for her.

Genny managed to swallow the lump in her throat knowing he wasn't angry or disappointed with her, not to mention there was no blame for what happened. It was as if the weight of the world had been lifted from her shoulders.

"My balls hurt, son of a bitch kicked me, but otherwise I'm good." He held up a bandaged hand. "He bit me too. Should've known that Willard was a sneaky street rat. How's Gid?"

"He's sleeping. The doctor said he lost a lot of blood, but he's strong and healthy. No fever either, which is a miracle." She laid her head on his shoulder. "I'm so sorry, Lee."

He pulled her over to the wall and sat her down. "You have nothing to apologize for. Your mother is fucking loco, and I thank God you left her at twelve or you'd probably be the same way."

Genny's reminder that Lee knew exactly what lay in her past made her cringe. "I'm sorry I didn't tell you the whole truth about me."

He squatted in front of her and cupped her cheek. "You did what you had to, Genny. You were just a girl when you had to become a mother. You're sure Sophie isn't Henry's, right?"

"No, she's not."

"Thank God. Henry was such an ass." Lee's comment made a chuckle bubble up inside her.

"That he was. Is everything going to be okay between us?" She held up her left hand, the gold band bright against the pale skin.

He took her hand and kissed the finger holding the wedding ring. "Darlin', there ain't nothing in this world that could keep me from being your husband. I love you and I meant every word of that vow we said last night."

"Thank God." Genny dropped on the ground next to him and hugged him so tight, she heard her own bones crack.

"I hate to interrupt, and I mean that, but we have a problem." Jake's voice permeated Genny's happy bubble.

"What is it?" Lee stood, hauling Genny to her feet more quickly than she thought possible.

"Margaret came over to let us know there was a stranger at the restaurant asking for Genevieve Boudreaux." Jake pointed at Genny. "That's you, right?"

Genny's heart began thundering again. "Yes, until last night anyway."

Lee squeezed her arm. "Where is he?"

"Zeke went and fetched him, put him in the jail. You need to take Genny over and find out what this man wants. Zeke sent Martin over to relieve you." Jake turned to leave as Martin, the burly blacksmith, appeared with a shotgun in hand.

With only a nod to the big man, Lee led Genny toward the jail. Her stomach clenched with fear over whoever she'd find at the jail. More blood could be spilled over her past coming back to cast its dark shadow over her new family. She just wanted it all to go away so she could start her new life with Lee. That wasn't going to happen of course—Genny had to face down and conquer her own demons.

"Are you sure you want to stay married to me?"

Lee stopped short and hauled her against him. His lips were hard, almost bruising in their intensity. "Until the day I die."

Genny could only nod, still wondering how such a grumpy one-armed man had come to mean the world to her. God really did have a strange sense of humor. After throwing so many obstacles in her way, He chose Lee to be hers. A man she loved who loved her in return.

Now if they could only get through the tangled mess of her previous existence in New Orleans, they might have a chance at happiness.

Lee promised himself if the stranger at the jail was anything like Willard, he'd shoot the son of a bitch between the eyes. He didn't want to bring Genny near the man, but no doubt he had already been stripped of his weapons before being thrown in the cage at the jail. Although the bastard couldn't physically harm her, he could damage her already battered heart. Her haunted eyes told a sorry tale Lee didn't want to add any more pages to.

They had all made it through a night from hell and survived. Thank God Gideon was doing well. That was at least a blessing for all of them. By the time they got to the jail, Genny was almost running to keep up with Lee, but she didn't say a word. He stopped at the door and ran his hand down his whiskered face.

197

"I'm sorry, Genny. I didn't mean to drag you like a plow." He punched the side of the building. "It's just, I can't—"

She put her fingers against his lips. "Don't apologize to me. I want this over with more than you do, so let's just get in there and see what other ghosts are going to appear from my past."

Lee had his suspicions that whoever the stranger was, he'd followed Camille. The woman was like a magnet for evil critters, a pied piper the rats followed. No doubt this man was a big rat out to do Genny harm. He was in for a big surprise then.

Zeke was leaning against the desk, pistols in their grips, arms folded across his chest. The stranger was in the cage pacing. He was tall with sandy brown hair cut short—an average-looking man who could be anyone.

"I've told you time and again, I ain't here for trouble. I am looking for Genevieve Boudreaux." He stopped pacing when he saw Lee, then his mouth dropped open when he saw Genny. "Genny, is that you?"

Genny sucked in a breath and put her hand over her mouth. "Bernard?"

The man smiled. "You look so grown up I hardly recognized you."

Who the hell was he? Before he could ask, Genny was at the bars with a smile on her face. "I never expected to see you again." She turned to Zeke. "Open this please. He's a friend."

Lee didn't appreciate the way her face lit up like the sunrise, the way she looked at him, the way the man looked at her. Lee's stomach cramped and he wanted to throw her over his shoulder and hide her.

Zeke gave Lee a questioning look, but he unlocked the cell. The tall young man swooped Genny into his arms and hugged her tight. Lee didn't even realize he had growled until Zeke put a hand on his arm.

"She's your wife, Lee. Step back." His big brother's voice was low but got through Lee's haze of pure jealousy.

Genny turned to Lee with a smile as wide as he'd ever seen on her face. "This is Bernard Mitchell. He worked as the stableboy at my home in New Orleans. When I was growing up, he was my only friend."

A friend. Judging by the look on Bernard's face, he didn't think of her as just a friend. The man was madly in love with Genny—Lee knew the look well because he saw it in the mirror every day.

"I'm so glad you're all right. When you went off in the night, I tried to find out where you went, but your mother wouldn't tell me." Bernard put his arm around her shoulders.

Lee's blood began a slow boil. Genny must have seen something in his face because she extricated herself from Bernard's arm and walked over to Lee. When she tucked her hand into his, the anger receded enough for him to think straight.

"Then how did you get here now?" Zeke voiced what Lee was already thinking.

Bernard looked back and forth between them. "Who are these men, Genny?"

Genny squeezed Lee's hand. "This is my husband, Lee Blackwood, and his brother, Zeke."

"Husband?" Bernard's face visibly fell and Lee felt no small amount of satisfaction that his new wife had made their relationship clear to the man from her past.

"That's not important, Mitchell. Start talking or your ass is gonna rot in that jail." At that moment Lee could have kissed his brother. Zeke sounded like the cool, hard sheriff perfectly.

"I-I saw Camille leaving. She packed almost everything she

owned within a day. And she left in the middle of the night. I heard her say your name, Genny, and I knew she was going to wherever you were." Bernard swallowed. "I couldn't help you eight years ago, but I thought maybe I could help you now. I know why she's here."

Genny's hand tightened on Lee's. "She told me she's here to visit me and my daughter."

"No, she's here to take your daughter back to New Orleans."

"What?" Genny swayed toward Lee. "Why would she do that? She hasn't cared enough to even write one letter in eight years. She didn't want me as a daughter, why would she want her granddaughter now?"

Her voice had risen to nearly a scream. Lee led her over to the desk and made her sit down. He kept his eye on Bernard, whose gaze was locked on Genny.

"What else do you know?" Zeke crowded Bernard, pushing him back into the cell. "Camille and her piece-of-shit boy tried to kill my fucking cousin. So you'd better tell us what you know or get the fuck out of my town."

Bernard looked like a rabbit facing the big bad wolf. Lee almost smiled at the sight, but then he remembered the dire situation they were in. He had to stop thinking about himself— he had a family to protect. No more selfish shit.

"Your daughter's name is Sophie, right?" Bernard glanced at Genny.

"Yes, her name is Sophie. She's...seven." Genny's ashen complexion worsened.

Bernard blew out a breath. "She is Allen Coddington's child."

It was a statement, not a question, but Genny nodded just

the same.

"Sirius Coddington must know about her somehow. He's offered your mother ten thousand dollars to bring her back to New Orleans to be raised in his house." Bernard's words dropped like rocks in a still pond.

"Excuse me?" Her mother had lied about Sirius's death, that was obvious. It was one of thousands of lies Camille Boudreaux had spouted. Instead of falling to pieces, the shocking information seemed to make Genny's spine straighter.

Bernard nodded, even as he tried to move away from Zeke's bulk. "It's true. I heard her talking to Sirius last week. She assured him she could retrieve the girl without any resistance."

"He knows where we are?" Genny's voice grew sharper.

"No, Camille refused to tell him. After all, if Sirius knew where Sophie was, he could send his men to get her." Bernard shook his head. "I think she wanted to feel the cash in her hand when she brought the girl back."

The man's appearance smacked of conspiracy with the very bitch who had arrived in Tanger to wreak havoc with their lives. Lee grabbed him by the collar, shaking him until his teeth rattled. "And now you appear in Tanger and tell us a story about Camille."

"I swear, I'm not working for her. I am Genny's friend, that's all." He swallowed so hard, Lee heard the man's throat move.

"I don't believe a word of it," Zeke spat.

"It's true. I swear." Bernard looked at Genny. "Genny, I came to help you. Eight years ago I didn't do nothing to help and you got sent away. I-I thought maybe I could make up for that."

Lee looked at Zeke and he realized his brother was thinking

the same thing. "Put him back in the cell."

Bernard sputtered as Zeke shoved him in the cell and turned the key. Genny turned to frown at Lee.

"What are you doing?"

"He's lying, Genny. Lying through his fucking teeth." Lee touched the gun on his hip. "If Naomi wouldn't yell at me for making a mess, I'd put a new hole in his head."

Bernard's eyes widened. "Don't let him shoot me, Genny."

Lee smelled raw fear coming from the man. Soon enough he'd tell them what they wanted to know.

"Lee, please. I don't think he's lying."

"You haven't seen him in eight years and he appears the day after your mother does telling you that he's here to help you? Think about it, Genny. He probably came with Camille to help *her*."

She finally heard what Lee was saying and this time when she looked at Bernard, her eyes narrowed.

"Bernard, what are you really doing here?"

This time, Bernard's innocent expression fell and guilt replaced it. "She promised me a thousand dollars to help her. Miss Boudreaux told me she needed help to get your daughter. I told her no, so she fired me." Bernard peered at her through the bars. "I'm sorry, Genny. So sorry. You've got to believe me. I only wanted to help you." Bernard sounded sincere, but Lee didn't believe him entirely.

Zeke looked at Genny. "It's up to you, sister. What do you want to do with him?"

She turned to look at Lee. In her eyes he saw confusion and fear, but he also saw something else. He realized she'd already forgiven Bernard and wanted his approval to let him out. Lee never thought he'd be able to communicate with a woman without words. Suddenly he knew he was in trouble, because he was always going to give in when she asked him for something, with or without words.

"Let him out, but the little bastard is not going to leave our sight." Lee was pleased when Genny smiled at him, a shaky one but a smile nonetheless.

"Don't worry, I'll shoot him if he tries anything." Zeke bared his teeth at Bernard and the young man looked like he would piss himself in a moment.

"Let's go back to the mill and see what's going on. I want to check on Gid." Lee took Genny's arm, confident his brother would keep the fool in check.

The sun had risen in full while they'd been at the jail. The warm sun couldn't chase away the chill that had settled in Genny's soul when she discovered the full extent of her mother's perfidy. She had used everyone around her for her own purposes, even to the point of plotting her granddaughter's kidnapping.

It made Genny wonder if she ever knew who her mother was at all. Camille had seemed like a vapid, self-centered woman but she'd shown herself to be more than manipulative. She'd crossed the line to cruel and crazy, with an insatiable need for money.

When Lee, Zeke, Genny and Bernard walked into the mill Jake rose from the table, the gun instantly in his hand. "I don't remember inviting him into my house."

"I did." Lee ushered them all in, much to Genny's relief. "This is Bernard. He's a, well, he's..."

"He's an old friend from New Orleans." Genny rescued her husband from telling her sordid life's tale to her new family. "He also told us why Camille is really here and will help us stop her."

Jake stared at Bernard a bit longer. "I'll let him take breakfast with us, but I ain't trusting nobody from New Orleans."

Genny couldn't blame Jake for being suspicious. She had a hard time figuring out how to trust herself. Bernard sounded sincere, though she wasn't sure she believed every word of his story. However he did sound earnest about what Camille planned. Or maybe she just wanted to believe her childhood friend wasn't another one of her mother's playthings.

The fact remained Camille had lied so many times Genny had lost count, and Sophie was now in serious danger.

Genny suddenly noticed Gideon was gone. "What happened?" Her gaze swept from Gabby to Naomi, but they both smiled.

"Don't worry. Gideon woke up and had a little broth. Jake and Martin carried him upstairs to recover. We just made some breakfast for everyone." Gabby gestured to the table. "Please sit. There's plenty."

Breakfast was a somber meal in comparison to dinner the night before. Genny could hardly remember what life was like two days earlier when her thoughts were on the wheat crop and finding a way to tell Lee she loved him. Now they were fighting for their lives.

"Camille wormed her way into staying with Hettie." Jake made a face. "That old bitty never liked me or Gabby as mayor. Did all she could to kick us off the town council."

"Wait, your wife is mayor?" Bernard stopped with a forkful of eggs halfway to his mouth.

"Is that a problem?" Jake narrowed his eyes.

"No, just, ah, surprised." The newcomer wisely turned his

attention back to his plate.

"If Camille is at Hettie's house, we should invite her to the restaurant for dinner. All of us can be there to confront her, arrest her and be done with it." Lee almost growled his plan. "I want this over with. I've already had a helluva wedding day and not much of a wedding night."

Genny squeezed his arm. "I think that's a great idea. Confronting her is the only way to bring her out into the open and finish whatever it is she started. I won't give her another chance to take my daughter."

"Then I can arrest her." Zeke's smile could have frightened small animals.

Genny never thought she'd be glad to see her mother again, but if they did this right, it would be the last time.

After some heated discussions, Genny left the mill with Lee, Zeke, Bernard and Jake. Gabby kissed her husband goodbye as if he was going to battle, which in a way, they all were.

Genny started trembling the moment her feet hit the porch. It wasn't excitement or fear, but rather the knowledge all the lies she'd based her life on were about to come crashing down, and along with it, the architect of her unhappy existence.

Jake walked with Bernard, keeping his hand on his pistol at all times. Genny barely noticed anything around her as she walked between Zeke and Lee. Together they were pretty formidable men, broad-shouldered, hats pulled down low, and lethal pistols strapped to their thighs. She felt safe, which was an unusual and unfamiliar feeling.

"I'll go to Hettie's house and meet you at the restaurant." Zeke broke off from the group and loped off down the side street to the house surrounded by flowers. It was as if Camille was the insect hiding in the beautiful blooms.

Margaret welcomed them into the restaurant. "Is Gideon all

right?"

Lee pulled out a chair for Genny. "Doc says he's got a long road, but he'll recover."

"Thank God." She glanced at Genny's finger. "Something you need to tell me, Lee?"

For the first time since he'd married Genny, Lee felt his cheeks heat, as if he had gone behind Margaret's back to marry another woman. Silly notion, but just the same, he couldn't stop it once it started.

"Genny and I got hitched yesterday." He squeezed his new wife's hand.

"Congratulations." Margaret smiled and Lee was pleased to see Genny smile in return.

"Thank you. Now can we get some coffee? I need some of that mud you brew." Lee hadn't teased her in so long, it felt surreal to do so.

Margaret picked up on it immediately. "At least the spoon doesn't stand up in it like that sludge you used to make."

With a chuckle, she went into the kitchen for coffee. Bernard and Jake settled at the table, and they turned together, watching the door, waiting for the spider to come into the trap they'd laid for her.

Genny just hoped no one else would get hurt. It was only through the grace of God that Gideon had survived the stab wounds. She would spend a great deal of time making it up to him with baked goods made from her own wheat.

It seemed like hours until they heard footsteps on the front steps, but it was only about ten minutes. By then the coffee had been drunk and the mood had tightened until the tension in the air almost crackled. When Genny heard Camille's voice, she nearly jumped off the chair. Lee put his hand on her knee.

"It's okay, darlin'. We're not going to let her hurt anyone again." He squeezed lightly and stood to face the woman who had come to destroy their lives.

Genny rose too, standing on his left side so Lee had free access to his gun. As soon as Camille walked in she nodded at Genny, ignored Lee, then she finally noticed Bernard. Her expression filled with rage and she looked between them.

"What is going on here?"

"I'd like to ask you the same question, *Maman*. Bernard has told us quite a few things about you and what you've come here to do." Genny's heart beat so hard her ears hurt, and her mouth went dry as cotton. She pressed on though, eager to vanquish the real demon in her life. "You were going to steal Sophie, weren't you? My daughter! She's the Coddington heir and you were going to bring her back to New Orleans for money. Tell me, *Maman*, did you honestly think I'd just give you my daughter? Or that I wouldn't fight you tooth and nail?" Genny was so furious she was nearly breathing fire.

Camille's face tightened until she resembled a hissing snake. "I thought to collect money from the brat I whelped twenty years ago. You ruined my life, my figure and cost me my inheritance."

"How dare you blame your stupidity on me?" Genny shook her head. "You chose to follow your lover to New Orleans."

"Ha! And you believe that story?" Camille circled the table in front of them, drawing closer to Genny. Zeke was ten feet behind her, gun in hand. "Your father was a stableboy. I made up the story about your society father so he would support me. You see I'd bedded him, but only after I'd caught pregnant already." Camille's smile was all sharp teeth. "I should have gone to that crazy voodoo woman and gotten rid of you when I had the chance. You've been nothing but trouble since then."

Genny tried to take it all in, but she felt as though Camille was slapping her with words. "*Maman,* I don't believe it."

"It doesn't matter what you believe. All I want is that girl." She pulled a pistol from her bag and pointed it straight at Genny. "Or you will leave her an orphan."

Genny stared down the mouth of the gun, its black muzzle a yawning maw of death. "My family is all here, including my husband. Will you kill us all?"

"I don't need to. All I need is to threaten you and your darling husband will do anything I want to save you." Camille cocked the gun. "Tell the sheriff to go get Sophie now or I will splatter your brains all over your new husband."

Lee was rigid as steel beside her, his breath coming in shallow pants. He'd risk his life for her, she knew that, but she refused to allow it to happen. If there was one thing she'd do right in her life, Genny would not permit someone she loved to be hurt again.

She stepped in front of Lee. "Go ahead and shoot me then, because I won't let you take Sophie."

"Genny!" Lee tried to get around her, but she widened her stance to block him.

"Come on, *Maman,* are you just big threats or are you going to use that gun?" Genny walked toward her until the gun pressed into her belly, hard and deadly against her. "Kill me. Or would you rather it be more dramatic?"

She didn't think about what she was doing, she couldn't. Genny only knew she had to stop her mother. She pulled the gun up until it was pressed against her cheek.

"Do it."

Camille cocked the gun but before she could pull the trigger, a sound of unholy terror broke the air. Genny dropped to her knees as the rebel yell echoed through the building. Zeke tried to pull the gun from Camille's hand, but she held on, firing into the air. The smell of gun powder and fear permeated the room. Genny got back up and ran at them, determined to stop her mother from hurting Zeke.

A strong arm snatched her by the waist, stealing the breath from her body just as Zeke hit the floor with Camille in his arms. The gun went off again. This time it didn't fire into the air. Genny screamed, unwilling to believe Zeke had been shot because of her. She struggled against the arm that held her captive, recognizing Lee's scent as he held her tight against his chest.

"Easy, Genny, easy."

"Oh my God, is Zeke hurt? I can't, please, he's your brother." She sobbed as the reality of another death hit her.

"No, he's not hit, but your mother is." Lee held her until she stopped flopping like a fish on a line.

Genny took hold of her self-control with both hands and yanked back at the panic and raw fury that had driven her. She'd tried to protect her new family, the only ones to ever accept her as she was, flaws and crimes included.

"My mother?"

"Yes, darlin'. I think she was hit in the chest." Lee let her down and took her hand. He rubbed at the gold band on her finger.

Zeke rose from the floor, blood splattered on his shirt. "She okay?" he cocked his head toward Genny.

"I think so, but she scared the shit out of me two minutes ago." Lee spoke of his wife as if she wasn't holding his hand, staring down at her mother's body.

Genny knelt and took her mother's hand, pressing it to her

cheek. "I'm sorry you didn't find your way to a family like mine, *Maman*. Finally, *se finis*."

"My God, Genny, are you okay?" Bernard appeared beside them, his face pale. "I've never seen such a thing before."

"Shut up, Mitchell, and help me take the body over to the doc's." Zeke didn't wait for Bernard to stop sputtering. The two of them, along with Jake, took Camille's body wrapped in a tablecloth, leaving Lee and Genny alone in the restaurant.

The blood on the floor was a stark reminder that death came to everyone, even those who deserved it. Genny could not feel bad for her mother's fate even if her childhood had shaped her into the monster she became. Somehow though, Genny had escaped from her mother's dark world, found a farm to call home, and finally a man to call her own.

Lee folded her into his embrace and Genny wept silent tears for her mother, for the childhood she never had, and for the grief she should feel for the woman who had given birth to her. Finally, finally, Genny was free.

They walked arm in arm out of the restaurant. Lee was glad Genny's mother was dead, but he wasn't going to tell her that. It wasn't very Christian of him, but hell, Camille wasn't much of a Christian woman herself. The woman had been a monster and he'd wonder for the rest of his life how she was blessed with an incredible daughter like Genny.

Lee wanted to take her home and start their life together.

Home.

Lee had a place to call his own, a farm that he would find a way to pay for no matter what. Even if it wasn't legally Genny's, they would keep it come hell or high water. By the time they arrived at the mill, Bernard was walking back with Zeke, eyes wide as he kept a wary eye on the big sheriff. He seemed so damn young compared to Lee, and there was likely only five years between them.

Bernard rose as they approached. "Genny, can I talk to you?"

"Only with me next to her." Lee glared at the man until he nodded.

"Of course, of course. I just wanted to ask if it was all right with you if I stayed here in Tanger? I don't have anything left in New Orleans, and well, this seems like a nice place to live." Bernard sounded so hopeful, even Lee felt himself waver.

"I think that would be wonderful." Genny turned to Lee. "Maybe he could work at the restaurant or the mill?"

Lee wanted to tell the man no, but it would have been damn rude. Genny was the voice of reason, and that's why they fit so well together. Her reason cancelled out his anger.

"Really? I appreciate it, Mr. Blackwood." Bernard held out a hand to Lee.

"Fine." Lee refused, however, to shake the man's hand. "I'm gonna tell you something right now and you need to remember this. If Sirius Coddington shows up in Tanger *ever*, I will hold you personally responsible. They will never find your body. You understand me?" He leaned in close enough to see the twitch in the other man's cheek as he absorbed Lee's threat.

"Yes, sir. I promise you, I didn't tell and I won't." Bernard turned his gaze to Genny. "I promise."

Genny smiled at him. "Thank you. Now go on inside and I'll be right there." She turned her back on Bernard and pulled Lee over to the side of the mill. The wheel was running and the spray of water, the thunder of the movement, echoed in Lee's chest.

She held his hand in hers and looked up into his eyes. "I

wanted two minutes alone with you. This has been the strangest, hardest two days of my life and that's saying a lot. You've stood by my side through the entire thing, believing in me, trusting me. I wanted to say thank you, to tell you that I love you so much it makes my heart nearly burst." Her voice caught on the last words and tears twinkled in her eyes.

Lee kissed the back of her hand then the ring on her finger. "You know, I think somewhere up in heaven my mother is looking down on her baby boy and smiling. Her ring was meant for your hand and I hope you'll wear it forever." He blinked away tears of his own. "I know I ain't fancy or handsome and my skills are limited to numbers and getting angry, but I love you too, Genny."

He pulled her close, feeling her heart beat against his. Lee had never felt such peace.

Their wedding night was two days late, but it arrived just the same. Genny was nervous, if that were possible. Sophie was long since asleep in her bed and Genny was getting ready to greet her husband in their marriage bed.

She used the warm water to wash from head to toe, then slipped on the silky nightdress Gabby had given her. Genny didn't want to ask where her friend had gotten the light blue concoction but it fit her like a glove.

Genny brushed her hair and looked at her reflection in the mirror. Her steady gaze looked back at her and for the first time since she could remember, there were no shadows behind her eyes. Loving Lee, letting go of the darkness of her past, had allowed her to finally be happy. A small knock at the door made her smile.

She stood and tried to smooth her hair but it wasn't cooperating. Ah, well, it wasn't as if it was their first time together.

Genny opened the door to find Lee standing there, shuffling his feet and looking nervous. His eyes widened at the sight of the nightdress.

"Hi there."

"Hi." He pulled a handful of wildflowers from behind his back. "I wanted this to be special."

Lee was so wonderful in his awkwardness, his attempt at wooing her. She took the flowers and laid them on the washstand, then took his hand, tugging him into the room. As Genny closed the door, she smiled at her new husband.

"Mr. Blackwood, it will be special for the rest of our lives." She trailed her hand along his shoulders, satisfied to see him shiver at her touch. "You have entirely too many clothes on."

"You, ah, have some interesting clothes on."

She laughed low in her throat. "I'm glad you like it. Now let's see what we can do here."

As she reached for his shirt, he took her hand. "No, tonight, it's my turn." He leaned forward and kissed her lightly. "Please."

Genny didn't know what he was up to, but she was willing to find out. He shed his shirt as quickly as he could. She kept her hands down although watching him struggle with the buttons with one hand wasn't easy.

"Your hair looks so beautiful." He ran his hand through the strands. "You know the first time I saw you I wanted to feel your hair against my skin."

Genny heard the truth in his words and closed her eyes as he stepped closer. His lips closed over hers in a gentle touch, then they grew firmer.

He cupped her breast and swiped his thumb across the nipple. It was her turn to shiver as arousal slid through her.

She swayed beneath his touch, eager to be together with him as husband and wife.

"This is so soft, almost as soft as your skin." Lee ran his hand down her back and cupped her behind, squeezing.

She gasped at the feel of his cock pressing into her belly. "Don't make me wait. Not now, Lee. Please." Genny took his hand and led him to the bed. "I want to be your wife in truth."

His smile was worth more than all the money in the world. "Your wish is my command, Mrs. Blackwood."

They shed their remaining clothes quickly and climbed into the bed until they faced each other. Genny put a hand on his chest and raised one brow.

"Let me love you." Her voice was low and full of need. She barely recognized herself.

Lee lay down, his hard staff lying on his belly, waiting for her. Genny's hand shook as she reached for him, but not from nervousness, but rather from the emotions flowing through her. Finally, finally, she was with a man who loved her, one who owned her heart in return.

She straddled him, sweeping her hair down his chest and groin. He moaned low and deep in his throat. With a smile, she did it again, her body heating with each pass. It was a heady feeling, knowing she was arousing both of them with just the light touch of her hair.

"You're torturing me," he choked out.

"You love it."

"I love you."

"I love you too." This time it was Genny's turn to be almost overwhelmed by the words. She slid forward and positioned herself above him, the head of his cock poised at the entrance of her pussy.

Their gazes locked as she lowered herself onto his staff inch by inch. When he was fully sheathed within her, Genny held her breath. They truly were made for each other, perfectly sized, perfectly matched.

Genny began to move, her body at one with Lee's. As she went down, he pushed up, their rhythm as perfect as their union. Her hair brushed his chest as she moved, and he let loose a groan with each touch of her locks.

"Genny."

"Lee."

Her orgasm began somewhere in New Orleans and traveled all the way to Texas, then up her legs and into her pussy, her heart and her soul. She exploded with the most unimaginable ecstasy, screaming his name as her body pulled his into his own orgasm.

It was a moment frozen in time, the perfect moment she would remember for the rest of her life. As the waves of pleasure began to fade, she lay beside him and felt tears prick her lids when his arm closed around her. Yes, now Genny was loved and loved in return.

Epilogue

"That's a lot of wheat." Sophie stood with her hands on her tiny hips and looked out across the golden fields.

"Yep, it sure is. It's not getting cut though with you jawing at me. Now are you ready?" Lee felt the weight of the cradle in his right hand and knew it was going to take at least two weeks of back-breaking labor from sunup to sundown to get the crop cut, dried and bundled.

She held up the twine. "Ready, Pa."

Lee could not believe the brat had taken to calling him pa. He wouldn't tell her it made his heart thump and his eyes sting, but he didn't tell her to stop either. They were going to use the money from this crop to buy the farm. Since they didn't have the cash, the wheat was going to be the rest of the money, along with Lee's meager savings, to really own their home.

Genny walked toward them, a jug of water in her hand and twine in the other. She set the jug down and shaded her eyes against the morning sun. "Someone's coming."

Lee peered toward the barn, noting a few wagons and horses. He didn't know what the hell was going on until he saw Zeke, Naomi, Gideon, Jake, Gabby and Bernard leading a crowd of people toward them.

The men were all carrying cradles.

"Sweet heavens." Genny's voice was full of awe and emotion.

This time Lee welcomed the stinging in his eyes. His family, the town he'd pushed away, they'd all come to the farm to help his newfound family bring in the crop. This was what he'd been missing all his life. The love of a woman, the sense of community, and the support of his neighbors.

"Who're all those folks?" Sophie stepped up beside them.

"That's our family, Sophie. That's our family." Lee swooped up his new daughter and put her on his shoulders, then took his wife's hand to go greet the town of Tanger.

Two lost souls, burned by the life they led, had found peace, love and happiness in Texas. One more Devil had finally come home.

About the Author

Beth has never been able to escape her imagination and it led her to the craft of writing romance novels. She's passionate about purple, books, and her family (not to mention long cruises). She works full-time and writes romance novels evening, weekends, early mornings and whenever there is a break in the madness.

She is compassionate, funny, a bit reserved at times, tenacious and a little quirky. Her cowboys and western romances speak of a bygone era, bringing her readers to an age where men were honest, hard and honkin' built.

For a change of pace, she also dives into some smokin' hot contemporaries, bringing you heat, romance and snappy dialogue.

To learn more about Beth Williamson, please visit www.bethwilliamson.com or send an email to Beth at beth@bethwilliamson.com.

In this game of hearts, winner takes all.

A Betting Chance
© *2010 Lynne Connolly*
The Triple Countess, Book 4

Sapphira Vardon needs five thousand pounds to avoid a cruel marriage and a grim future, and there's only one path for her. Don a mask and an assumed name, and risk everything to win at the gaming tables. First, though, she has to get through the door. Luckily she knows just whose name to drop.

Corin, Lord Elston, is curious to find out who used his name to gain entrance to Mother Brown's whorehouse and gaming hell. The enigmatic woman who calls herself Lucia isn't the sort of female usually found here. Behind her mask and heavy makeup, she's obviously a respectable woman—who plays a devilish hand of cards.

Sapphira is desperate to keep her identity a secret, but Lord Elston's devastating kisses and touches demand complete surrender. And once he learns the truth, there's more at stake than guineas. Corin finds himself falling hard for a woman who's poised to run. A woman who's about to learn that he only plays to win...

Warning: Hot action on the gaming table and in the bedroom might make you go looking for a time machine.

Available now in ebook and print from Samhain Publishing.

"I wish you'd trust me with your secret. I might be able to help," Lord Elston said.

"I don't know you." Not in any recognized meaning of the word. The connection Sapphira felt to him had to be her imagination. He couldn't feel it, not this wild needing.

"I think we should get to know each other better. I want you to trust me." He touched her chin, his forefinger stroking her skin. She wanted to purr like a cat, but instead she moved back. Before she could retreat out of his reach he tilted her chin up so she had to meet his direct gaze. His eyes bored into her soul. "There's something about you—I don't know." He bit his lip. It was the first time she'd seen any vulnerability about him and she found it meltingly seductive.

She couldn't risk weakening. She put her guard back up and kept it firmly in place, reminding herself that he was a stranger, that she didn't know him. "I told you, I can't do that. I'm here to play cards, no more."

"I love a challenge," he murmured, and lowered his head.

The first touch of his lips against hers paralyzed her. Recognition—of what she still didn't know—shot between them and she opened her mouth to protest, but he used it to his advantage and licked her lips before he slid his tongue into her mouth.

Now shock held her rigid. Nobody had ever kissed her like this. She hadn't imagined it possible. She'd seen the caricatures in the shops with their sometimes explicit content, watched a man fondling a whore, seen mercenary transactions take place in the street—she'd thought herself reasonably au fait with sexual matters, for a virgin.

She'd been wrong. She knew that watching and experiencing were two different things but had never known it could be so devastatingly different. The intimacy floored her, and she could do nothing other than reach out for something to steady herself.

The memory of that other kiss—that disgusting, slobbering kiss George Barber had forced on her—returned in full measure. This didn't compare, couldn't. She wanted to press closer to Elston, not jerk away, put as much distance between them as she could. Nothing like that. If anything had told her that she couldn't go ahead with marriage to George Barber, this did.

Corin cupped the back of her head as her hand made contact with his velvet-clad arm. She clutched it, praying for control as he took his time exploring her mouth, caressing her with soft strokes that made her heat up right down to the forbidden area between her thighs. He held her safe, didn't move his hands or try to unfasten her clothing. One arm curved around her waist, the other over her wig. She wanted his hands under it, in her hair, cupping her head intimately. One of the strings of her mask loosened.

She jerked back, her hand going to her only protection against discovery. "No, don't!" Her voice was breathless, whispery, but at least it still worked. As did her common sense.

"I want to see you." He sounded as out of breath as she did.

"No, you can't." She reached up and retied the one string he'd managed to undo. Luckily the other one still held firm. He'd dislodged her wig, and she pulled it back into place, but he must have seen that she was a brunette.

"Why not? Will I know you?"

Having regained her composure, enough to confront him anyway, she shook her head. "It's highly doubtful. But you might see me somewhere else."

"And you've lost that accent. I knew you'd assumed it, but there's still a tinge left. Are you a Londoner?"

Born and bred. "I've visited London a lot," she said, hoping desperately to put him off the scent. She had to get out of here before he guessed more. Before he had her out of her clothes and spread out on the bed for his pleasure. How could she have been so stupid?

But she had to pass him to get to the door, and he caught her skirts. "A challenge, sweet Lucia. Just between us."

"Why?"

"Because of the danger. Because you want a bit of excitement in your life." If only he knew she'd have more excitement than she'd ever wanted soon. But she appreciated that he didn't threaten her. He could have her barred from this house with very little trouble, but he hadn't done it.

She turned around, willing at least to listen, but keeping some distance between them, as much as this small room would allow. He sat there in his splendid clothes looking every inch a prince. A wicked prince. He released his clutch on her skirt, and she resisted the urge to put her hand where his had just been, to touch the residual warmth. "Well?"

"Let me get to know you better. You intrigue me. Can you meet me, talk to me, with your mask and maquillage off? Can you look me in the face without your protection?"

"No." She couldn't do it. With no mask or makeup he'd see every expression on her face, and he'd know she was his for the taking, however hard she fought against it.

He leaned back, smiling. "A challenge, then. A bet, just between us, with no money at stake. If I recognize you and challenge you in public without your disguise, you promise to meet me at a place of my choice."

"Why?"

He smiled. "I want you, sweet Lucia. I want to see your face while I'm making love to you."

Before she could repress it an image flashed into her mind. Him, naked, admiring her naked body, kissing it, touching it. Oh she wanted it so much, but she couldn't. Mustn't. She held back her shock. Barely. "And what's in it for me?"

His rich laugh filled the small space with joy. "I hope to give you pleasure as I'm taking it."

She pulled out of his grasp, put her hand on the door latch. "I can't." Then she was gone, hurrying toward her servant, Frankie, as fast as she could without colliding with anyone or losing her foothold.

LaVergne, TN USA
16 February 2011
216725LV00012B/2/P